RETURN TO Mariglenn

Book I
The Lost Stories Series

Return to Mariglenn

Return to Mariglenn was chosen by the Marlowe-Pritcher Estate trustee, Thomas Marlowe III, as the most fitting of the family Journals to share first with the public for reasons that will become obvious to the reader. Though primarily written by twelve year old, Jenny Habledean Pritcher (1855-1939), it is certain from the handwritten manuscripts that some editing was done when Jenny's writing style and penmanship were more developed.

The internal watercolor illustrations were likely rendered later and inserted into the text of the journal. The family believes that they are the work of Jenny's cousin, Katherine Pritcher.

We have made every effort to present Jenny's journal as she intended it, with limited corrections and formatting required for modern publication. Some section headings have been added for clarity.

The final manuscript has been approved by Thomas Marlowe III. Please refer to the continuation of our Publisher's Note and postscript at the end of this most unusual work.

Copyright © 2022 Thomas Marlowe III
All rights reserved.
ISBN: 979-8-9874759-1-1 (Paperback)
ISBN: 979-8-9874759-2-8 (Hardback)
ISBN: 979-8-9874759-3-5 (eBook)

Cover Design, Terance Lusich; uncredited images in the book are courtesy of the Marlowe-Pritcher Estate/Thomas Marlowe III, trustee

All rights reserved. No part of this book may be reproduced or transmitted in any form or by any means, electronic or mechanical, including photocopying and recording, or by any information storage and retrieval system, without the express permission in writing from the publisher.

Published in the United States by Old Dominion Press

Printed in the United States
2022—First Edition

We are not sure if this is true; however, it seems true, and if it is not, it should be.

SPECIAL SALES
Most Old Dominion Press books are available at special quantity discounts when purchased in bulk by corporations, organizations, and special-interest groups. For information, please email sales@OldDominionPress.com.

The Lost Stories

Return to Mariglenn

The Journals and Stories Of Jenny H. Pritcher

Return to Mariglenn includes the first of several journals and stories of Jenny H. Pritcher to be published.

CONTENTS

The Beginning *1*
A Real Town *6*
The Grand Adventure *8*
Oliver the Hero *18*
The World Has Changed *24*
Sailing to England *28*
Searching England For Cousins *34*
The Fall of Fallbright *39*
On to Scotland *47*
Mustard Seeds *52*
Return to Mariglenn *57*
The Highlands *60*
Key and Tassel *67*
Mountain Men *73*
The Caverns *77*
Wedding Cake *81*
Publishers Note . . . continued *85*

The Beginning

18 October 1866

In the spring of 1865, Grandfather Pritcher came home to Mariglenn. Father did not come home. He died on a hill in Pennsylvania. Pennsylvania is up north, but not as far north as Maine. I have a letter from a man who is now the Governor of Maine. He promised Father to write Mother and I, and though he is a Yankee I forgive him and think maybe God will forgive him, but Mother says she cannot forgive.

Dear Mrs. Nehemiah Pritcher,

As you are sadly aware your husband died at the battle of Little Round Top at Gettysburg, Pennsylvania. I was the last man to speak with him before he passed on, and to heaven without a doubt. He had no other on his mind excepting you and your daughter, and these were his final words as I penned them in my notes two days after that battle.

> *Please, Sir, forgive me. Please send word if you can to my wife and daughter in Hot Springs. Tell them they are as all the lights in the heavens to me. I am so sorry to leave them now. Tell them I was true to my friends and true to Virginia to the last. I think now that angels are coming for me. I reason we did not take the hill. We should have taken it yesterday but I have done my part. Sir tell my family I have done my part. I know not what else I could have done. And I assume, Sir, you have done your part and, no doubt as you hold the hill, done yours well. Tell my little Jenny if God wills she will yet have her grandfather. I do now see the heavens opening for me. Sir, Sir, God have mercy on us.*

I hope you ladies will also forgive me for my part. The struggle is now over and I wish you well in rebuilding your fair state and your lives.

Please excuse my belated effort in this matter, as it was brought to mind as I reviewed my notes of the war.

Very Respectfully Yours,

Joshua L. Chamberlain
3 September 1865

Mother says all the men have gone mad, especially Grandfather. Though I do not think him mad at all. He goes to see the Yankee from Rhode Island at the cabinet shop almost every day. Sometimes they come back to Mariglenn together in the evening and have supper and talk in the study by the fire until after I am asleep.

The Yankee man is really Mr. Marlowe, and he guarded Grandfather when he was captured by the Yankees. But Mr. Marlowe always speaks very kindly to me and sometimes asks me questions that I must think about.

Grandfather looks after Mother and I, and Mariglenn and all his business things. Mother says he does not task the help as he should and that the war has hurt his mind. But Hannah says the Lord has touched him.

Hannah is even older than Grandfather and has been at Mariglenn forever. I am teaching Hannah to read and write, which makes Mother a little sore, but Grandfather tells her to "leave it alone," that Hannah ought to learn letters if she pleases.

The boys in town tease me about Grandfather if they ever catch me alone. They say he is a secret Yankee. But Hannah says boys cannot be expected to know much about anything but mischief, especially the dirty barefoot hooligans that twiddle around Hot Springs. Mr. Marlowe says they tease me because I am so pretty, and I think he is right.

I am Jenny Habledean Pritcher. Grandfather calls me Jenny Sweetness. I was born May 5, 1855. My father was Capt. Nehemiah Pritcher and he was a very brave soldier in the war.

I like to write, so Mr. Marlowe has made me my own writing table and chair to match. The wood came from a great sugar maple tree at Mariglenn that was struck by lightning. Mr. Marlowe says the lightning is still in the wood and he could feel it as he worked the boards, and when the moonlight comes through the window my writing table glows silver and I feel I am far away.

Hannah told me lightning wood has magic and I think that Grandfather overheard, for he had Mr. Marlowe make Hannah a sewing box of the same wood and told Hannah when she mends his britches he shouldn't wonder if he would fly right off his horse.

Hannah is not to be bested in a tease and told Grandfather it would take more than a few magic stitches to float him off his horse, and said a magic girdle would serve smartly.

There is magic in my desk and my chair. I feel it now as I write and I cannot write well without them, but here as I am I can write on and on.

∽

20 October 1866

I asked the shop boy again today what Mr. Marlowe and Grandfather do in the back shop room. He told me again he did not know, as they never allow him to go in, but thinks Grandfather mostly sits and talks while Mr. Marlowe works at something. Whatever it is, they've been at it ever since Mr. Marlowe came to Hot Springs a year ago. I think it is the real reason for Mr. Marlowe coming.

Mother says it is foolishness for Grandfather to invite a Yankee soldier to Virginia and get him a shop and tools and set him up so generously. She says money ought to be spent rebuilding what the Yankees ruined, and not wasted setting up Yankees in business. But I hear some in town say Mr. Marlowe is the best cabinet maker in the state and has come from a grand cabinet making family in Newport. Mother says that's all the more peculiar why he should come to Hot Springs, where only Grandfather has the money to pay what he's worth.

I hear he mends chairs and cradles and things for poor folks that can't pay at all, and has little concern for collecting from anyone else.

Mother did not complain so much when Grandfather sent to New York for some new dresses for her and I, and told her it was time to set aside her mourning dress. We spent all afternoon trying things on and giving things to Hannah to alter. Mother talked about feeling guilty, but kept trying things on and asking how she looked. I asked if Grandfather was being wasteful giving money to dressmakers up north. She told me that no dressmakers ever came marching into Virginia shootin' things up and maybe it was alright what Grandfather had done.

Hannah tells us that Walter, who sees after the stables, heard that

Mr. Marlowe has been calling on Mrs. Melinda Taylor, who is a war widow like Mother, except Melinda Taylor is very poor and has twin boys.

Jonathan Taylor is as mean as a snake and kicks any dog he sees. I think he is one of the barefoot hooligans. His twin, Oliver, is the shop boy who helps Mr. Marlowe.

Maybe Mr. Marlowe will marry Melinda Taylor and put Jonathan on a short rope in the woodshop.

24 October 1866

Mother and I went to church today in new dresses. Everyone whispered about us. Mother put extra money in the pass-around basket and sang the hymns loudly. When we rode home the leaves were such a color as I cannot name. Walter says the sky was bluest blue. I want to write a poem about those leaves and that blue sky, but the magic in my desk and chair is not working now.

I think I'll go find Grandfather and Mr. Marlowe on the mountain where they often walk on Sunday.

A Real Town

12 November 1866

My Aunt Sophia and Uncle Randolf are visiting at Mariglenn. They've come from Staunton, which is a real town where they say trains may come soon. Sophia is Mother's sister. Randolf was also a brave soldier in the war, so the Yankees shot off his leg. They want me to come visit them for Christmas because they have no children. Mother is thinking about it. Aunt Sophia says I'm the prettiest child there ever was and that I read and write as good as most grownups.

I can open the Bible up anyplace and just start reading. I showed Aunt Sophia I could do it and now she believes I can, and asked Mother and Uncle Randolf if they could believe it.

Sometimes Aunt Sophia just puts her hands on my cheeks and kisses me and cries just a bit and tells me I'm the picture of Heaven.

I do wish I could have cousins or a baby sister. Mother could get married again, but I don't think she'll find any man to suit her, so my best hope is for a baby cousin.

15 December 1866

Mother will allow me to go to Staunton for Christmas. I am excited to go. I will meet Randolf and Sophia at the inn in West Augusta, where we will stop over. Walter will take me in the carriage that far, as Grandfather is gone to Fairfax until January. Grandfather is sad to be away at Christmas but has a lot of business there. Mother will not come to Staunton even though Aunt Sophia begs her. Mother says Sophia is trying to match make her and has some man in mind who is sure to torment her, and though she'll die to be alone at Christmas, she'll die three times in Staunton.

I heard Mother talking to Walter in the kitchen. She said she would give him a horse pistol for the trip and told him to shoot any man dead who so much as looked at me sideways. She told Walter if anything happened to me she was liable to shoot him herself. Walter said he'd as soon shoot as get shot and told Mother not to worry. But Mother seems very worried and tells me a hundred things to be careful of and to be on my best.

Mother says if the weather does not stay fair I may not go, but I've prayed fair weather will hold.

∞

28 December 1866

I am safely back at Mariglenn, having never seen Staunton, but had a wonderful, dangerous time. Hannah says I should sit right down in my magic chair and write it all up as a story so as my babies and grandbabies could know about it someday far off. Hannah says she'll sit down with me and we'll drink coffee and she'll mend all my clothes that got tore to pieces with things from her magic sewing box. Mother is sick in bed with bad nerves.

The Grand Adventure

*The Grand Adventure of My Peril and Rescue
and of Mother Almost Shooting Walter*

The weather was fair enough when Walter and I set out at first light for West Augusta to meet Sophia and Randolf. We rode north to Monterey, then east to McDowell.

It was eleven in the morning and Walter said he was miserably hungry, so we stopped at the battlefield in McDowell to eat what Hannah had packed. I was too excited to eat, so Walter ate everything in the basket.

I asked Walter why he did not leave Mariglenn like some when Mr. Lincoln set them free. Walter said he was waitin' to see which way the wind was gonna blow, and then, in blowed Master Pritcher all changed up, and changed up for the better as far as he could tell. He said he knew nothing but horses, that he was paid alright, which was more than what some white men in town could say. . . . He asked if I was satisfied with that.

I said I was very glad he stayed.

I asked what made Grandfather change so.

Walter said he guessed my Grandfather had seen so much hurtin' goin' on in the war and so many of his own men die like dumb animals, and maybe, too, all that about my father not believing in the war but going off to fight anyway, dying in Pennsylvania, not even being brought back to Mariglenn to lay down at the family grave site. Walter said this was his best reasoning, but anyone else could make their own guess, since Grandfather never spoke personal on such things to anyone but Mr. Marlowe.

I cried a little thinking of Father, but didn't let Walter see. He must have known, for he said my father was one of the finest men he knew, and that he only went to fight cause he knew there was no other thing on the green earth he could do but go.

The wind chilled quickly then, and Walter said we must move on. He cracked the whip at Charlie's ears and we hurried from the battlefield.

Walter seemed fretful when we passed Head Waters, for the wind was blowing cold from the northeast. The sky clouded over and looked full of snow. He switched Charlie and cursed. He did excuse himself, but looked more worried than ever. Then the snow came. Walter talked about turning back to Head Waters, but decided to go on.

Going down the mountainsides was more difficult than going up. The carriage slid and was jolted by rocks in the road. I held tight to the seat and saw Charlie slip. When he gained his feet again he bolted. Now Walter really cursed and didn't excuse himself. I thought the carriage would break to pieces. Walter screamed for me to hold on with all my strength. The snow was blowing so fine and thick we could not see, but I could hear the sound of a stream, and then Charlie raced right through it. We must have hit a big rock and stopped stiff, but Walter kept right on going, right through the air holding tight to the reins. Somehow I held tight, but nearly pulled my arms out of socket.

Charlie was sprawled on the far side of the stream and looked badly hurt. I could not see Walter at first. I climbed down into the cold water. The rocks were icy and I fell and got all wet before I crossed over. Then I saw Walter bleeding in the snow and moaning about how Miss Trudy (that's Mother) was going to shoot him to death. He could not see me as his eyes were filled with blood. I knelt by him and wiped the blood from his face with my skirts. When he saw me not dead or broke to pieces he thanked the Lord over and over. He was still bleeding badly from his head. I took my scarf and wrapped his head as I had seen in the church they'd made into a hospital during the war. His eyes closed and he seemed to slip away. I covered Walter with my wool cape, and then went to get some dry things in our baggage that was still tied well to the carriage.

Charlie was making awful noises and trying to lift his head. I slipped in the stream again before I reached the carriage. My fingers were frozen stiff and I couldn't untie the baggage. I began to cry. I was sure we would all freeze to death. I was listening for angels to come for me like they came for Father on the hill in Pennsylvania, but I could not hear angels yet, so I made it back to where Walter was lying. His eyes were closed but he was still breathing. I got the jack knife from his pocket so I could cut the ropes. Walter's knife was sharp and the ropes cut quick.

Before long I had Walter covered with my New York dresses and everything else in my bag. But now I was so frozen and had nothing else dry to wrap in. I thought maybe Father might yet come along with the angels to get me. Then I thought to cut the cover from the carriage.

I stepped again into the stream, which didn't seem so cold this time, and that's when I saw Oliver, the shop boy, riding down the hill on the bay mare. I wondered what on earth he was doing out there in a snowstorm. He walked the mare steady down the hill.

Oliver spoke calmly. "Mr. Marlowe is very sick; he would have come himself if he were not. Mr. Marlowe woke this morning saying he had a dream that you and Walter would run into terrible trouble. He sent me to follow you only a few hours after you left."

I asked him why Mr. Marlowe did not send a grown-up. Oliver said Mr. Marlowe knew no grown-ups that would do anything on account of a dream he'd had.

Oliver is older than me, maybe thirteen. I heard some boys his age fought the war. I took comfort at the thought.

Oliver crossed the stream and climbed off the bay where Walter was laid out. He took the blanket from under his saddle and wrapped me up. He took a hatchet from his pack and went to cutting limbs from hemlocks and gathering dead wood from the ground. He piled the dry wood in the snow near Walter, but not too close. He pulled a flask from his pack and poured it out over the pile of wood. I could smell it was kerosene. With one match the fire blazed. He told me not to stand too close and to turn around occasionally to warm my backside.

Charlie was still groaning on the ground, so Oliver went to the carriage and opened the sidebox. He took the pistol that Mother had given Walter. I closed my eyes, not wanting to see Charlie get shot, but I knew it was right because he suffered so.

Walter moved a little when the gun fired, but lay still again.

The snow kept falling but the wind had died down. I wanted to climb in the fire and curl up with the red coals. My limbs ached and I had not eaten since early morning and was hungry. Oliver had nothing but dry biscuits to give me but I was grateful to have them.

He gathered more wood and piled it near the fire. He turned Walter around gently to warm him all over and checked the wound on his head, giving a wondering look at my New York dresses all piled on him.

"I think his collar bone is broken, and who knows what else," Oliver said.

"He'll sure to die if we try to move him. We'll build a shelter right here by the road with the fire in front 'til more help comes."

Then Oliver took the blanket from me, which had become wet from the melting ice on my dress. He took the faded blue wool cape from off his shoulders and draped it over me. I pulled it close around me and stood as close to the fire as I dared. I thought then that there was no need for the angels to come for me now since Oliver had come. I was very happy to go on being alive.

It was snowing harder than ever and what little light there was faded away. I kept the fire blazing while Oliver hacked out poles and hemlock boughs for the shelter.

Earlier on Oliver had hitched up the bay mare to the carriage harness and pulled it behind us to block the wind. He piled boughs against it to make a fine wall.

Late into the night Oliver kept on hacking and building, hacking and building, all around Walter and I. I rearranged as best I could and made Walter a nice bed off the ground. I changed his head bandages and brought him a little water from the stream to drink. He awoke now and then from dreams about Mother shooting him with the horse pistol. He was confused and screamed for us to "put out the fire, that the barn was burning down."

Finally, Oliver stopped building. He had even built a little stable for the mare and gave her some cracked corn from the sack Walter had brought for Charlie.

When Oliver came into our shelter I said nothing about how hungry I was, but he must have known. He supposed I would not want to eat Charlie, but said that he had eaten horse meat a time or two but never a horse that he knew. I was so hungry I thought I could eat a horse, but I could not eat Charlie or even bear to go see him lying dead in the snow.

Oliver had the big pistol stuck in his britches. He warmed himself next to me at the fire that blazed at the open end of the shelter. He had found a bottle of blackberry wine that Walter had stashed in the carriage box; he pulled out the cork with his teeth and handed it to me. It was sweet and cold but warmed me on the inside. I drank a generous bit and gave it back to Oliver. He took a more generous helping and I laughed a bit, seeing him with that big pistol in his britches and drinkin' out of the bottle. I laughed a bit more, thinking what Mother would say if she came upon us just now. Oliver smiled for the first time since he'd come when he saw me laughing. He gave me back the bottle and told me to go easy on it. He said he might arrange venison for breakfast, and took the sack of cracked corn and disappeared into the snow and the darkness.

While Oliver was gone I changed Walter's bandages again. He was sleeping more peaceful and had no fever. The snow kept falling and was now knee-deep. The wind was up again and smoke sometimes filled the shelter. I made a good floor with hemlock boughs and set out the baggage to make seats for Oliver and I.

Oliver returned and told me he had spread some cracked corn a ways down the road, and that if deer were anywhere about we might have some breakfast.

I must have fallen asleep sitting on my trunk but woke at the sound of the pistol shot. I sat awake tossing wood in the fire and watching the blackness turn gray beyond the flames. The snow was very deep now and still falling hard. Charlie was nothing more than big white mound, and the only sound was the stream running off the mountain and on past our little camp.

[I read all that I have written aloud to Hannah and asked her if she likes how I'm writing the story. Hannah says she can see it all perfect like a vision and for me to go on writing away.]

Finally, I hear the sound of Oliver pushing through the deep snow. Looking through the cracks in the shelter I see a harness strap over his shoulder and dragging behind in his tracks are slabs and strips of bright red meat. I stepped out in front of the shelter to show I was awake and ready to help. Oliver was still sportin' the horse pistol in his britches and seemed mighty pleased with himself. I told him I could eat it all and for him to bring it right in. I said since he did the huntin' I ought to do the cookin'. He agreed and handed me a long round strip of meat. He said it was the tenderloin, and "the best eatin' there was." He told me to push some coals off to the side of the fire and turn it slowly with a spit. Oliver made me one quick with a sugar maple limb. He ran the pointy end longways up the middle and handed it over to me.

While I was turning it over the coals Oliver went about piling up snow against the sides and back of our shelter. He hoisted the rest of the meat up over a sycamore branch that hung high over the

The Lost Stories

stream. He said this was to keep the bears from having it. I could no longer see through the cracks in the walls as they were now covered by the snow bank. The smell of cooking venison must have slapped Walter out of his painful sleep. He awoke groaning but his mind was clear."What's goin' on Jenny? What's that smell? Has Randolf come for us?" he asked.

Oliver came in and told Walter to hush and lie easy. He told him that only he had come and we didn't expect anyone else soon in waist deep snow.

Walter lay silent for awhile then started on about how Oliver ought to just shoot him now and get it over with. He said Miss Trudy would shoot him sure enough back home and if Oliver shot him now it would save him a painful ride home in the back of a buckboard. I told Walter right then that I did not patch him up and spoil all my fancy dresses on him just to let Mother shoot him when we got home.

I said, "I'll protect you and won't let Mother harm you worse than you are now. When we get home you lay up in your room at the stables; Hannah will know how to mend you; just make yourself scarce 'til I've got Mother set straight. I'll stand between you and Mother if I have to, Walter. I give it my solemn word."

That calmed him down some but the rest of the blackberry wine calmed him more, and when he was finished drinking it straight down, we gave him a little meat. We all ate roasted tenderloin for breakfast and then cooked a shoulder for dinner.

It kept right on snowing all day and into the night. Oliver kept on banking snow against the shelter walls 'til we were snug as we could be. Walter teased that Oliver should keep right on going and build us a stone chimney and maybe a few rooms up top. He said he was tired of venison and would like some beans and pork and cornbread with apple butter, and he would be happier if we'd fluff his pillows more often.

Oliver went right along with him and said it would all be done and would there be anything else. Walter said in truth there was one kindness we could do him. He said we weren't as good a snoops as we thought we was, that he had something a shy better than blackberry wine in a jug wrapped in an oat sack in a saddle box in the carriage. He told us it was for special painful occasions of the body or soul, and though Jenny's promise of protection had eased his soul somewhat, his body was having extra special pain.

Oliver asked if that was smart since he'd lost so much blood. But Walter assured us he would administer the remedy in proper doses.

The next two days were mostly spent gathering firewood, cooking venison and listening to Walter sing or lament about how he let his life's true love get stolen away by his no-count cousin Nathan.

The snow finally stopped and by noon of the fifth day of our trouble, Randolf and two other men arrived from West Augusta in a logging sleigh and a team. Randolf wept to see us safe and admired our shelter and told Walter he looked very fine with my dresses pulled up to his neck.

One of the men was a surgeon in the war and offered to have a look at Walter.

Walter said, "Thank you much, Sir, but I intend on gettin' dragged out of here with everything I came in with," and that the man should keep his saw in his bag. Walter said he was under the protection of Miss Jenny and Mr. Oliver and would soon be cured up by Doc Hannah, and thanked the man again. Randolf and the other man laughed at this but the doctor got red in the ears.

Everything that was worth saving was loaded up on the logging sled. Walter was carefully lifted and loaded in as well. I rode seated in front with Uncle Randolf, wrapped in a great bear fur, and Oliver was sent ahead to tell Mother all was well.

Mother was waiting on the front terrace crying and thanking the Lord for protecting me. She was scolding herself for ever letting me go and especially with that fool Walter. Walter hid completely under his blankets in the back of the sleigh. I told Mother that Walter did his best and it could have been worse. I said Walter had suffered enough and was very near dead already, and there was no use in her shootin' him.

Mother said she'd decide later whether to shoot him or not and took me inside. When she took the bear robe off me and saw the condition I was in she dropped right to the parlor floor. Hannah and Randolf tried to revive her but it was no use. They took her up to bed and she's still there now. I go to see her every morning and read to her from the Bible. I just open it up and read, and let the Lord decide what verses will help her most. This morning I opened to Leviticus and read about all kinds of unclean things. This seemed to calm her down, for she went straight back to sleep.

The End

~~~

5 January 1867

Grandfather has returned and brought wonderful presents. He has given mother a train ticket she can use to go anywhere she wishes. The ticket says she may ride the train however often she likes through July: Grandfather says Mother needs to air out a bit.

For Hannah he brought a set of fine silver ink pens and a matching ink well. There was a box of the best writing paper, too.

He brought tins of tobacco for all the hands and a fine new suit for Mr. Green who runs the house. There was something for everyone. But Grandfather teased and said he had nothing for me, that he had shamefully forgot to get me a gift, but he would go right back to Fairfax and get me something if that should please me. I said it would not please me for him to go away ever again. He liked my answer very much, then remembered that he had brought me a present after all, but I could not have it 'til I told him all about my grand adventure with Walter and Oliver.

Everyone came into the parlor by the fire, except Mother, who excused herself. Grandfather had Mr. Green pour wine all around. I read from my writing book the whole story. Grandfather slapped his knee at all the best parts. He especially admired the way Oliver took such care of us. He told everyone he would give Oliver that horse pistol as a Christmas present, and invited us all to go visit "Walter the invalid" in his room to share our wine with him.

So everyone but Mother marched down to the stables to cheer up Walter, who cheered up nicely, and was very glad to hear that Oliver was going to get the pistol.

Hannah told Grandfather that Walter had not a broken bone in his body and was just a bag of bruises and that he was just a whiny baby. Walter was wounded by Hannah calling him a baby, so Hannah mentioned the terrible cut on his head to give him a little credit.

The rest of the evening was happily spent and when Hannah finally walked me to my room, Grandfather followed and said he would like to see me alone before I went to bed. I expected this as he had not yet given me a present. Hannah teased and said I was much too tired and she must tuck me in directly. I carried on with Hannah, saying I was too tired to spend time with forgetful old men.

"Well then," said Grandfather. "I won't detain you." And he turned and headed back down the steps.

"Come back!" I screamed. Grandfather turned about and opened his arms. I jumped right over three steps and Grandfather caught me.

"My my.... eatin' all that wild venison has affected you, Jenny Sweetness," Grandfather said, and he carried me up to my room and pretended to huff and puff like I was a big sack of potatoes. He set me down in my magic chair and turned me about to face him. He got down on his knees and told me to hold out my hand. I did, and closed my eyes even though he didn't tell me to. Then I opened my eyes and saw in my hand a plain brass key with an emerald green tassel. Grandfather said it was the key to the greatest thing in all the world, and for me never to lose it. Grandfather then kissed me sweet on my forehead and left my room.

Oliver the Hero

7 January 1867

Grandfather said that I could give the big pistol to Oliver if I promised to make a proper show of it. Hannah says Oliver is a great hero and even if he should prove to be a no-count scoundrel the rest of his life that he might get past St. Peter just for saving her Jenny Sweetness. Hannah said she didn't know if saving Walter would count a stroke for Oliver or against him, that the Lord would judge on that.

17 January 1867

I waited for Walter to be off his bed so he could take me to the wood shop to give the pistol to Oliver.

Hannah sewed up a fine velvet wrap and Grandfather had Mr. Marlowe make an oak case. I waxed the case myself. There is a black wood band around the lid and an oval picture painted with milk paint in the middle. The picture is of a young man with a drawn sword pointing at the sky at a snow storm shaped like a dragon. He has a royal blue cape blown back by the terrible snow dragon. He is protecting a beautiful girl (who looks like me). There was no more room in the oval to paint in Walter, but Walter says he doesn't mind.

I wore my best fancy dress. When Hannah saw me setting up in the carriage she said I could take the breath out of a hurricane. Grandfather said Amen.

When we got to the wood shop, Mr. Marlowe pretended to be surprised. He made a big show and laid out a roll of muslin for me to walk from the carriage to the door. Oliver was shocked. I walked up to him at the work table. I knelt right in the sawdust and asked him if I could rise up. He said of course I could. When I rose up and looked at him I could see I was getting the effect I planned on. I handed him the pistol case, kissed him on his cheek then turned and marched back to the carriage. Mr. Marlowe helped me up then gave me a proper bow. Walter and me rode straight back to Mariglenn.

The Lost Stories

18 January 1867

Mother is very upset about the show I put on giving Oliver the pistol. When she heard I knelt in sawdust she turned white. She said she was grateful as everyone else for Oliver's help but saw no need to put on so.

Mother says the whole house is gone mad, that we have no thought for the example we're putting up. She says we need to keep up our proper pride despite what the Yankees have done to put it down. She said that Grandfather might have a keen mind for business but he's keen on nothing else.

I asked Mr. Green about why Grandfather was so good at business. He told me that if old Jefferson Davis had left the money matters to my Grandfather that Dixie would be as rich as England and could have hired out for others to do the fightin'. He said leastways there'd been no barefoot soldiers or lack of powder and ball. He said Grandfather had business things going on all over the world and maybe a thing or two on the moon.

I asked Mr. Green if we were rich.

"Lord have mercy, child" was his answer.

He told me not to worry myself about Grandfather's business.

I told him I wasn't worried a bit, but just liked to know what there was to know. I asked who would take care of Grandfather's business when he passed on now that Father is gone. I told Mr. Green that I already knew that Grandmother died when my Father was born and it was a shame she had no other babies except Father because I would love to have cousins. Mr. Green hung his head when I said this. He seemed very sad, too, that I had no cousins. I told Mr. Green that Mother said that Sophia and Randolf could not have children because of Randolf getting so hurt in the war. Mr. Green said he heard that was so. Then Mr. Green brightened up. He knelt down and whispered to me. He said I should go up to my magic writing desk and write up a letter to Grandfather saying that cousins is what I want most in all the world. I asked what good that could do. He asked if I could keep a secret. I flatly told him I could not. I told Mr. Green that secrets jump out of me so fast I have no chance to enjoy having them, but I would try my best. He said that would do.

Mr. Green thought a minute, then said, "The world is all new to you, Jenny Sweetness. I know you think you might never have cousins, but what does the Bible say about that little ole mustard seed, all about moving mountains. I'm just saying that if you write up that letter to Colonel Pritcher, maybe the Allegheny Mountains might all jump up and do a jig for you."

This was the strangest thing I have ever heard Mr. Green say, and I'm reconsidering what Mother says about everyone going mad around here, but still, Mr. Green is the most straight up of everyone. I'd count it all off if it was said by Walter or one of the hands, but that Mr. Green says it has me hoping just a bit. I don't know if my little bit hope is equaled up to a mustard seed of faith, but I did dream a dream last night that the mountains were all singing and dancing and an old oak tree was playing the fiddle.

I don't know what that means, but I'm gonna try that letter to Grandfather

3 February 1867

<u>My Letter to Grandfather and How All the World Changed Because of It</u>

Dear Grandfather,

I hope you will not think I am foolish or a silly girl who knows nothing about anything. You may set aside this letter but I pray you will not think poorly of me.

I know I should never have cousins unless a doctor can fix Randolf, which Mother says cannot be done. I know that Grandmother died when Father was born. You see, I know the way everything is. I am not writing to you because there is anything that can be done, but just so you know what I am feeling inside, since you often ask how I'm feeling and what I'm thinking.

I'm writing it all in a letter because I could never get it all out saying it right to you. Not that I am not a good talker, it's just that I am a bit unsure about what I want to say

But as you can see, I've given you back the tasseled key that's the key to the best thing in all the world, because I would trade all the

21

best things in the world if I could have real cousins or even just one cousin, even if it was a boy.

And also I had a dream that the mountains were singing and dancing and an oak tree was playing fiddle. I thought you might need to know that.

*Your Granddaughter,
Jenny*

P.S. *As you can see, I took care to write in my best hand with Hannah's silver pen and good paper, which she freely offered when she heard of my intentions. I thought that might count for something.*

J.P.

❦

I copied my letter to Grandfather in my book so maybe my babies and grandbabies would know about believing in something just a tiny bit and what might happen if they do something about it.

And what did happen was this.

A few days after I gave Grandfather the letter he called everyone into the parlor after supper. He told Mother to please sit down because he didn't want her falling down. He had me sit in the middle of the red velvet settee and he sat next to me.

Grandfather explained about my letter and how he thought Mr. Green and Hannah must be in on it somehow. He said perhaps I was now old enough to understand regardless of what anyone else might think. Grandfather looked at Mother when he said this and Mother was getting very nervous. Then Grandfather turned to me and held my hands in his.

"Jenny Sweetness, you don't have to give up anything to have your cousins. Your Father did have a brother who was twelve years his elder. His name is Benjamin. When Benjamin was a very young man, no older than Oliver, he and I had a terrible fight. I was a very hardheaded man back then, Jenny, and I did a very foolish thing. I told Benjamin to leave Mariglenn and never come back. I didn't mean it when I said it, but just said it to sting him."

Hannah was standing by the door and began to cry when

Grandfather got to this point. Mr. Green and Grandfather went over to give her a kerchief. Mr. Green was getting choked up too, but Mother was staring right out the window into the cold night and hardly breathing. Then Grandfather had Hannah sit next to me on the settee and I stroked her hand to comfort her.

Grandfather went on. "But Jenny, your uncle Benjamin turned about and went down the lane running. He ran past all the maple trees, which were on fire with autumn colors. I watched him run 'til he was out of sight. And Sweet Jenny, will you and God above forgive me, but I have never laid eyes on Benjamin since."

Finally, Mother fell right out of her chair onto the Persian rug, I was thinking, as Grandfather was telling about Uncle Benjamin, that I should put down some cushions for her to fall on, but I was busy comforting Hannah. Grandfather said just to leave her lay 'til he had said what he had to say.

Grandfather went on. "The hopeful part is that Mr. Marlowe's sister in Newport has married an Englishman. The man once worked at a bank in London which held an account of a man by the name of Benjamin Pritcher. He wondered if he was any relation to the Pritchers of Hot Springs. Mr. Marlowe told me this just before I went to Fairfax, knowing full well about Benjamin because I had confided the incident regarding Benjamin to him when I was a prisoner in the war. Now I have no idea if this is our Benjamin or not, but I intend to go myself to London and find out. I know I could hire a firm in London to investigate for me, but I feel I must do this myself. And Jenny, since you are so eager about cousins, I'd like you to go with me, unless your mother has any objections. Do you have any objections, Trudy? Ah, see there, I didn't think she would mind. "Would you like to go to England with me, Jenny?"

"Would I ride a train?" I asked.

"Yes, and a beautiful sailing ship as well."

"Then I suppose I will go."

Well that was that. The world had changed. And Grandfather and Mr. Green carried Mother up to her bed.

The World Has Changed

25 March 1867

I am writing now in my book while riding a train from Charlottesville to Alexandria. Grandfather and I will sail from there to England to see if the London Benjamin is our Benjamin and to see if I have cousins. Grandfather speaks as if he is not sure, but I know he is my uncle. I have a whole fistful of mustard seed faith about it. I can already see him looking just like Father. When he sees me he will say what a lady I am. But I suppose he will say it fancy like an Englishman. With me right there he will have to forgive Grandfather. Then he will invite us to meet his wife and all my cousins who will all talk fancy as well. That's as far as I can see right now.

All Virginia is swooshin' by so fast out the train window I can't even appreciate it. I've seen some towns that look pretty shot up and burned. Grandfather knows all about what happened in those towns and in battlefields we pass. He talks of it with other gentlemen on the train.

When we left Mariglenn, Grandfather gave charge of everything to Mr. Green. Mother has not left her room or spoken since learning about Benjamin.

Hannah told me to bring back my cousins to Virginia and she'd love 'em all up just like she done me. She told Grandfather if anything happened to her Jenny Sweetness that he might as well not come back and go on sailin' 'round the world 'til the Lord come again.

Walter told me to watch out for pirates, and that he'd pray a whale didn't swallow up the boat.

When Walter left Grandfather and I at the station in Charlottesville, he said he'd be waiting there in the selfsame spot when we came back to take us all home. He told us to make it quick 'cause he'd get miserably hungry waitin' for us.

27 March 1867

I am now in Alexandria. Our ship sails the day after tomorrow. Grandfather has lots of business to take care of and I go with him wherever he goes. Everyone asks if I am the Jenny they have heard about. They say I am more lovely than even Grandfather's boasting could tell.

One sweet lady asked if I should like a grandmother. She said if I did not keep a close watch on my Grandfather that I might have one. I said I should love to have a grandmother and I would close my eyes so Grandfather could be snatched up. She said I had a sharp wit. I told her I knew my wit was sharp, that it came from my Hannah who could match wits with the three wisemen. I told her about where Hannah goes to church, that all the people there say Hannah is like a prophet in the Bible and they all listen close when she speaks. I told her that even Grandfather and Mr. Marlowe listen to her mindfully and she often gets the last word. I also told her I was teaching Hannah to read and write so she could write up in a book all the Lord was telling her.

The sweet lady asked me if Hannah had ever visioned Grandfather getting married again. I told her I did not recall Hannah saying anything about that.

This afternoon we rode the carriage to Georgetown. We had dinner at a gentleman's house that was all stuck up against other houses on a rough stone street.

There was a boy there and he was very polite to me and wore a fine suit. He said he would have his father's bank someday. I told him that I would soon have cousins which I never had before. I told him he looked very smart in his suit.

28 March 1867

Today Grandfather took me to many shops in Alexandria. We bought dresses and shoes and matching umbrellas. Grandfather says it will rain a lot in England in the spring. I asked if there would be much lightning. Grandfather thinks not.

It was warm in the afternoon so we had cakes and coffee in an outside cafe. I asked Grandfather if I should have a grandmother soon. He asked if I would like to have a grandmother. I told him though I've never had a grandmother I would feel greedy asking for a grandmother when I've just been given cousins. Grandfather said we could not be sure at all if I had cousins in England. I said that I was sure that I did.

"Well, then," said Grandfather. "I will not spoil you by giving you a new grandmother as well." I told him that would be alright, that I should not want to be spoiled.

Then a strange thing happened that I do not understand.

After coffee, Grandfather took me to a shop which was filled with beautiful jewelry. He waved his hand around and told me I could have any one thing I wanted. The shopkeeper was very pleased. Grandfather said that all his business was done until our ship sailed in the morning and that I could take my time deciding.

"Anything?" I asked.

"Absolutely anything," he replied.

I had something very different in mind than the shiny jewelry. I supposed I would look fancy to my new cousins with a ruby necklace or maybe pearls, but they might think I was spoiled and would not like me.

"I want to know what Mr. Marlowe is making in his back shop," I said.

The shopkeeper was not pleased with my choice. Grandfather was silent a moment and then took my hand and led me out of the shop. I took his arm and we walked slowly up the street. The sun was down and the lamps were being lit. As best as I can remember, this is what Grandfather told me, and I will always remember it because Grandfather spoke so strangely.

"Jenny, Sweetheart, you are such an unusual child. The Pritchers have always been odd, but you are without guile. You know so little about life, yet so much about love. Or perhaps I don't even understand you, Jenny. I have seen so much badness. Maybe I cannot see you aright. But I love you so much. I will not tell you how lovely you are because everyone tells you. Ah, but I will. I will tell you how lovely you are. You are as lovely as Virginia once was. Green, green Virginia. Virginia was a kingdom, a shining green kingdom. In his back shop Mr. Marlowe is making the ocean. He is making the little mountains that hide the highland valleys. He is building a busy town and carving the rivers that run to the bay. He is crafting all my dreams and all that I've forgotten. Mr. Marlowe is building a quiet early morning so that I may give it all to you and your children when I am gone to the night."

When Grandfather finished he put the emerald tasseled key back into my hand.

Sailing to England

6 April 1867

Our ship is now in the ocean sailing to England, but I do not feel well and cannot write much.

10 April 1867

Today I am feeling better and have gone about the ship a little. Grandfather says I will soon have my sea legs. I told him I would much rather have a sea belly, for that is the part of me the worse off.

I do love our cabin on the ship. It is so small, but has everything we need. There is a window and sometimes the sea rises up and covers it so that I cannot see the sky. I am not afraid, I know the sea will bring us up again, for it always does.

11 April 1867

Grandfather says that this evening we shall dine with the Captain. I will wear a blue dress to show the Captain that I have no bad feelings because he was Captain of a Yankee warship.

I met the Captain and his daughter today. They are from Philadelphia, which is Pennsylvania, which is where my father died. I did not tell this to them for they were so kind to me.

The daughter's name is Clara, and she is eighteen and soon to be married to a man in Philadelphia.

Clara said that my Grandfather had a mill near Philadelphia and two others in Baltimore. I told Clara I did not know about that. But I told Clara we were going to England to find my cousins and my uncle, who had been lost for a long time. She said she was sure we would find them and that they would certainly all fall in love with me the moment they saw me. I told her I was planning on that, and also to bring them all back to Mariglenn, which is their real home.

Clara wondered if perhaps my cousins had a grandpa and grandma in England and would be sad to leave.

Late evening, 11 April 1867

I talked with Clara all during dinner and hardly ate. Grandfather allowed me a little wine, but I had a good bit more than he allowed, which seemed to help me go right on talking with Clara 'til it was late. Then Clara took me all about the ship which was lighted by lamps in some parts but only by the moon and stars in others. She introduced me to members of the crew who always took off their woolen caps and made us a little bow, but not a bow like gentlemen, but like Mr. Marlowe or Walter, who do not bow often.

14 April 1867

Today the weather is stormy. Father is with the Captain and Clara is with me in our cabin.

I've shown Clara my writing book and she tells me she has a book, too, and calls it her diary and has gone to get it. She told me she has never let another soul read it but will allow me. I told Clara she could read my book too, if she liked.

Later 14 April

It is very late. Grandfather is asleep and is making lots of noise as he does when he sleeps, and I have awakened.

I did not light the lamp, for the moon is shining so brightly off the water and through the window. It is like when the moon shines off the snow at Mariglenn when I can look out at night and see the fields and the orchard and every tree along the lane and even the tops of the mountains are lighted, though the hills in the ocean move and the light and shadows change about as our ship rolls upon the water.

I am glad I have awakened so I can write about this day that Clara and I had together.

Clara allowed me to read from her diary aloud while she sat and laughed and blushed. I thought life in Philadelphia was very different from life at Mariglenn. Clara knows so many people. I could not keep them straight. She writes about dances and handsome men who wear uniforms. Clara has brothers and cousins and two grandmothers and one grandfather and also the man she will marry, who was a Yankee officer but who did not fight much in the war. Her two brothers were too young to be in the Army and Clara is grateful for that. Her father sailed a warship about the coast *"to keep the Rebels from getting guns and supplies from Europe."*

Clara loved to hear me read aloud. She said my little Virginia voice made her writing sound so silly and that was fine because Clara said she knew she was often a silly girl. But Edmund, the man she would marry, did not know how silly she was.

Clara said she'd always wished for a sister and perhaps I should like to be her sister.

Then I let Clara read from my book. She only laughed a little and even then, through her tears. When she read Governor Chamberlain's letter about when Father died on that hill in Pennsylvania, she cried and could not stop. She held me to her breast and said that I was a wonderful child and said she was very sorry about Father.

Later, Clara teased me a little about Oliver, saying that he might someday seek his fortune then come back and marry me. I didn't understand why Oliver should need a fortune to marry me, but Clara thought Oliver could not marry me otherwise.

Clara loved Hannah most of all and asked if Hannah was a slave. I told Clara I did not understand about slaves, but had heard so much talk about them that I was confused.

I said that Hannah was just Hannah and she had always been at Mariglenn but she never had a husband or children. I told Clara that Hannah was a grandmother and a mother to me, and that my mother had bad nerves and worried for me, but was not strong like Hannah. Hannah was like the mountains and the giant maple trees.

Clara said I had a way with words so that she could see all that I wrote about. She said she could even see in her mind my grandfather floating off his horse in magic britches made for him by Hannah.

I asked Clara if she believed my writing desk and chair had got a little magic from the lightning. She said she was sure that they had magic and asked if I had not been struck by lightning as well. I knew she teased me, so I told her that I once danced in the orchard during a thunderstorm 'till was so filled up with magic from being hit by lightning that I could turn myself into a falcon or a fawn or even a muskrat if I chose.

Clara then told me that I should jump overboard, turn into a big fish and swim on ahead to Liverpool.

I had such a time with Clara. Tomorrow if the weather is fair we shall have tea in her cabin, which has a very large window, and shall talk about whatever we please.

Clara asked me so many questions I cannot remember them all. But of all her questions I especially remember this. She asked why I wrote in my book that Grandfather was a prisoner in the war and was guarded by Mr. Marlowe. I said that was what I was always told. She said it was not exactly true, but not exactly untrue. So I asked her to only tell me the true part because I like to know things.

Clara told me that Grandfather was not a Colonel in the Southern Army but a General. But that people oftimes call him *Colonel Pritcher* because he was a Colonel for the Army before the war, and only ever wanted to be called that by his friends. She said she thought he did command in many terrible battles, especially in Virginia. But the main thing he did had something to do with England and trying to get everyone to stop fighting. Clara said she heard ladies and officers whispering about my Grandfather often at parties or at tea. She said that Grandfather was never a prisoner like other prisoners and that Mr. Marlowe was not a guard like other guards. But for the last year of the war Mr. Marlowe escorted Grandfather wherever he went. . . . Even to England.

I told Clara that it was very interesting to know about that.

༺༻

15 April 1867

The wind is very strong today and the ship leans hard to one side. I am in Clara's cabin having tea and cakes, which she says I must learn to do regularly if I am to go to England. Clara wants to watch me write in my book to see if sparks come from my fingers as I write. I tell her to excuse me, but I must be at my own desk to write anything magic, and that otherwise I write very ordinary.

Clara says that if she had a magic desk and chair she would write wonderful love letters to her Edmund. I tell her that would be a wonderful waste of magic. She says I should write a letter to Oliver my hero, and tell him I love him and will marry him when he has made his fortune.

I tell Clara that she must think of something else to talk about.

Clara tells me that her mother died when her father was away at war, and that her mother was her closest friend. She says that her mother wore herself out fretting about father at sea.

"She had a burning fever for days then died while all the house slept and could not even say farewell."

Clara is not crying. She is looking out the big window. I am looking out the window with her. We are seeing the wind whip across the waves. The sea is gray and white.

I tell her I am sorry and that she should tell me more about her Edmund.

~~~

20 April 1867

The Captain says we will be in port at Liverpool before the end of the month.

I learned today that the ship we sail on belongs to Grandfather as well as the cargo. I heard Captain Johnson and his first mate talking outside Clara's door. I asked Clara about it and she said she did know about that.

She asked if I did not know how wealthy my grandfather was. I told her I knew he had lots of business everywhere and some people say that he is rich, but I knew little of his business.

The crew calls the ship the *St. Anna*, but they say it will have a new name when we sail home.

Grandfather complains that Clara is keeping me all to herself and that he hopes I do not forget my old Grandfather. I pretend I do not hear what Grandfather says and ask him what will be *St. Anna*'s new name. He says that he is too lonely presently to remember what name he has chosen and that I should ask him later. I tell Grandfather that he should not name the ship *Jenny Sweetness* for I would worry about it all the time. Grandfather says he was not considering that name as it is very bad luck to name ships after neglectful granddaughters. I go and kiss Grandfather's long sideburns and tell him he should not pout so.

4 May 1867

We are now in London. I had never imagined such a busy place. There are so many horses and carriages in the streets. There are grand houses and shops everywhere and so many ladies and gentlemen. There are rough folks, too, and I cannot understand them when they talk. It is even sometimes hard to understand the well dressed people, but I am learning.

We rode a train from Liverpool to London. Clara and I had a happy farewell because we know we shall sail back to America together on Grandfather's ship.

Captain Johnson is taking care of all the ship's business and Clara is going to stay with friends in the northwest. Clara's friends have a home in the country near a large lake in the county of Cumbria.

Grandfather has told Capt. Johnson that we shall not sail back home until he has either found Benjamin or is convinced that Benjamin is not in England.

Grandfather has told me to pack only a small bag and that we should leave all else at our hotel here in London. He says we shall possibly be moving about very quickly and wants little fuss. I will bring riding clothes and my green wool cape.

Grandfather says I should bring one lovely dress, so I have chosen one that is pale yellow with white lace because the weather here is dreary and all I see is green and gray. When I find my cousins I think yellow will cheer them.

I am leaving my writing book here in London, but will tell all that happens when I can.

15 June 1867

I finally have the chance to write all that has happened since we left London.

Searching England For Cousins

By Jenny Habledean Pritcher

The search for Uncle Benjamin and my cousins began at a bank in London that was as grand as a palace.

Grandfather went to speak to the president of the bank while I waited in another room with a man who pretended to be very busy, but seemed to have very little to do.

I told him that his bank must have lots of money. He said the bank did not really have money but that it took care of other people's money. So I asked him how the bank got all the money to build such a grand building. This upset him and he told me that little girls from Southern America couldn't possibly understand modern banking.

Then he pretended again to be very busy at his desk while I waited for Grandfather.

Finally Grandfather came out of the big office looking very sad. He asked me to take his arm. I could feel him trembling, which scared me, for I have never known Grandfather to tremble. He thanked the bank president and the man who sat with me and we walked out of the bank. Grandfather said nothing to me, but raised his hand to hail a carriage. It began to rain so we opened our umbrellas.

We were very surprised when an older man came up behind us. He asked if he could share my umbrella, as he had rushed out of the bank without his. He asked Grandfather if he was indeed Mr. Benjamin Pritcher Sr. When Grandfather said that indeed he was, the man apologized for the misunderstanding in the bank. He said he had been the bank president's personal secretary for five years and was also secretary to the previous bank president for twenty years.

He told Grandfather to disregard whatever had been told him in the bank, and not to give up his search. He said for fear of losing his post and pension, he could say no more, but wished us luck and Godspeed. He then ran from under my umbrella through the rain and back into the bank.

Grandfather gripped my hand firmly and his face brightened again. I asked if we should go back into the bank and try to discover the truth. Grandfather said we could not, that he would never want to endanger that good man who had given us hope.

When we were in the carriage I asked Grandfather what was it that the bank president said that we should now disregard. He told me that the man told him that he could not give out information concerning the bank's patrons; though he could say that the Benjamin Pritcher who indeed held accounts at the bank was assuredly not an American, nor ever was, that he was from a very established family in Avon County near Bristol.

We rode in the carriage back to our hotel and Grandfather had the driver wait for us. Our bags were brought down and we then rode to the station and boarded a train for Bristol.

It was night when we arrived at the station in Bristol. We walked through the fog to an inn near the station. Grandfather asked the innkeeper's wife if she knew of a Benjamin Pritcher who lived out in the county. She said that Bristol was a big city and she had never heard of any Pritchers, but that didn't mean much. She asked if the Pritcher fellow was in any sort of trouble and perhaps the police could help or the sheriff of Avon. Grandfather said there was no trouble, but the sheriff at Avon might still be able to help. The lady explained how he could find the sheriff. Grandfather thanked her and asked if we could be wakened early.

It was still dark when the innkeeper knocked at our door in the morning. Grandfather asked him to hire us a carriage for the day. He told the man that we wanted a driver that knew the county well and who could spare us the entire day.... Grandfather added simply, "We will pay him very well for his trouble."

Within a half hour we settled with the innkeeper and were being helped by the driver with our few bags. He was one of those English people who is hard for me to understand. He said he'd heard we were from America and we were looking for someone. Grandfather explained to him that we were looking for the Pritcher estate out in Avon County. The driver said if there was any Pritchers in Avon, we'd find 'em sooner or later. Grandfather told him he was just the man we needed and gave him a five-pound note, which must have been allot by the way he looked at it.

"Tell me what we know?" said the driver.

"What is your name, sir?" Grandfather called back to him.

I'm Albert Sands, but mostly I'm called Wiggle."

"Well then, Mr. Wiggle, we know that the Pritchers are a respectable family near Bristol in Avon, and that's it."

"The respectable part narrows it down a bit. People of property, are they?"

"We assume," Grandfather answered.

Mr. Sands cropped his horse and we were off through the dirty town of Bristol.

The rest of the day was spent bouncing in the carriage seat and stopping at every pub that Mr. Sands knew of in the county, and he seemed to know exactly where each of them were.

Everyone knew Mr. Sands and called him Sir Wiggle. I asked him how he got that name and he answered. "You don't wanna know, Missy" I told him my name was Jenny Pritcher and we were looking for my Uncle Benjamin and all my cousins.

"We'll find 'em, Missy," said Sir Wiggle.

"I'm Jenny," I reminded him.

"Yes, Missy, you did say that."

Sir Wiggle stayed a little while in every pub he went in, to ask about the Pritchers. I think he refreshed himself each time as well. He began to sing a silly song about hunting for Pritchers that went like this:

"Pritchers, Pritchers, up in the dale,
Pritchers, Pritchers, stuck in a pail,
Pritchers, Pritchers, sure to find,
Pritchers, Pritchers, just my kind."

He made up many different verses, all to the same tune, with every line starting with "Pritchers, Pritchers."

I thought Grandfather might be upset with Wiggle's song, but Grandfather told Wiggle he had a real gift for rhyme and even helped Wiggle out if he was stuck for a good word.

Grandfather told me not to worry, that Mr. Wiggle was employing a methodical searching method that would produce results sooner or later.

It was beginning to get dark. I did not know where we were, as it seemed to me we were going around in circles.

Mr. Wiggle stopped at another pub and Grandfather gave him a pound note and said, "Good work, man. You're as good as a bloodhound."

Grandfather had to help Mr. Wiggle down from the carriage and steady him. Mr. Wiggle could not make his songs rhyme well anymore so he made up words so it would be easier.

"Pritchers, Pritchers, hoogledy doo,
Pritchers, Pritchers, stuck in a shoe,
Pritchers, Pritchers, klickedy klick,
Pritchers, Pritchers, schmikedy schmick."

In a few moments, Mr. Wiggle came out of the pub and answered, "I've found Pritchers!"

"Where?" asked Grandfather.

Wiggle pointed down the road. "It cannot be missed. Fallbright Hall, a ways down."

"Perhaps, Wiggle, you would like to stay here, as we have private family matters to attend and we wouldn't want you waiting out in the chill night. If you trust us with the carriage, that is."

"I trust you like you was my granny. You and Missy take all the time you need. I'll be right here when yer through."

"I trust you certainly will be, and thank you so much, Mr. Sands You've been ever so helpful," Grandfather said.

I went and took Wiggle by the arm and led him into the pub. The room was lit by a large fire and candles above the bar. A kind lady helped Wiggle to sit down. I told her that Mr. Wiggle was very tired and needed to rest. That he had been searching for my cousins all day, but now we have found them.

She said, "Is that so, Missy?" I told her that I was not really Missy. That was Wiggle's special name for me.

"I'm Jenny Pritcher and my Grandfather is Benjamin Pritcher and we are from Virginia, in America."

She only said, "Steady your heart, sweet Missy, steady your heart."

I did not understand what she meant. I walked from the smoky room and back to the carriage where Grandfather had taken up the reins and was waiting. He helped me up, then we were on our way to Fallbright Hall.

We turned in at a great stone arch. Iron fence lined the lane with pickets like arrows pointing skyward, leading toward the manor ahead in the darkness.

I drew close to Grandfather on the carriage seat. The spring night was chilled and I could hear thunder coming closer. Before we arrived at the house, the rain fell hard and lightning lit the treeless fields. All the outer buildings and barns had roofs of thatch which flashed amber blue in the lighting.

I could see no light from the windows of the vast stone house, which looked more like a fortress. Lightning cracked above the roof and frightened our horse, who jerked at the harness then backed away twisting and stamping. Grandfather tried to steady him while I opened my umbrella.

Grandfather screamed for me to go and knock at the door while he tried to keep control of the carriage, which he stilled long enough for me to climb down. Before I reached the door, the wind snatched my umbrella from my hand and whipped my hair furiously. I grabbed the large iron ring from the jaws of the iron lion and banged the door. I waited in the wind and the rain but no one came. I banged again and began to cry. I was frightened and excited and wanted my cousins to open the door for me.

"Uncle Benjamin!" I screamed. "Uncle Benjamin!"

The Fall of Fallbright

I reached again for the iron ring and just as I grabbed hold of it, the door swung open and hurled me over the threshold and onto the cold stone floor.

Out in the storm I could not see Grandfather or the carriage, and before I could turn to see who opened the door, the door slammed shut.

At first all was darkness, but I knew someone was close, then the lightning flashed and for an instant I saw the man. Long dark hair and wavering eyes. In the darkness again, he came close and whispered to me.

"What do you want?" He smelled like Mr. Wiggle and I thought he'd been refreshing himself too much. The lightning illuminated him again standing up and leaning upon a cane with a mean dog's head. "What do you want?" he said loudly.

"Are you my uncle?" I asked the blackness.

"Who are you, child? What do you want?"

"I am Jenny Pritcher, and I want my Uncle Benjamin and my cousins."

The man said nothing for a long time. Twice the lightning flashed, first showing a face confused upon an unsteady frame, then a sloppy arrogant smile.

"I know what you're about, little missy. You must think me a great fool. Well, whoever put you up to this is the fool. Benjamin is nothing, he has nothing, and your little show will avail you nothing."

I heard another voice, from down the hall, calling, "Master Pritcher, what is the problem?" The light of a candle was moving toward us and a woman's voice called again, "Master Pritcher, is all well, Sir?"

"Well enough, Cook. The storm has blown in a bold little imposter who's been put to the task by a monstrous idiot."

"Dear heavens, child," said the woman. "Where are your parents?"

"My father was killed in the war and Mother is back at Mariglenn in Virginia." I was trembling terribly.

"She's faltering a bit, but does quite well with the accent," said the man.

"Have mercy, Master Pritcher. What do you know about the girl?"

"I know I want her out of my house and off my property."

"Master Pritcher, perhaps you would like to go back to the study and let me tend to the child."

"Yes, you best tend to her, Cook, or I'll tend to her with my stick."

When he said this, he struck the steel tip of his cane at the floor and sparks flew at his feet.

I was still sitting on the floor when the woman came over and knelt by me with her candle. She wrapped her shawl about my shoulders.

The terrible man yelled from down the great hall where he staggered.

"Get her out, Cook. I want nothing wasted on her."

"Are you alright, child? Did Master Pritcher hurt you?"

"I'm just wet and I've lost my umbrella in the wind. I think the horse bolted and I'm not sure where Grandfather is."

"Who is your grandfather, Miss?"

"My grandfather is Benjamin Pritcher."

"Sweetheart, what are you talking about? Benjamin is gone and he certainly has no granddaughter. Now come with me to the kitchen. This hall is like a tomb."

Cook led me down the hall and past the study where the man sat slumped in his chair before a fading fire.

"Is that my Uncle Benjamin?" I asked as we passed.

"You must be frightened out of your wits, child. You're talking nonsense. Please hush now, Miss."

"I'm worried about Grandfather," I whispered to Cook.

"I'll send someone to find your driver. Now follow me please, Missy."

I followed Cook down the wide hall then down a curved stone staircase.

The kitchen was warm and water boiled in a large kettle upon the stove. Cook lit two lamps and the room glowed. Wonderful smells wrapped around me like the smells in our kitchen at Mariglenn before our cook left to get married a year ago.

"I'm going to get us some tea, sweetheart, and I want you to calm down and tell me what this business is all about."

Cook pulled on a cord hanging down the wall and in a moment a young lady came into the kitchen.

"Catherine. Go find Mr. Wells at the stables and tell him there's a carriage and driver on the property having trouble in the storm. Tell him to take care of the carriage. And I want you to bring the driver here to the kitchen."

"Yes, Mum," Catherine said, and hurried out the back.

"You are from America," said Cook "I can tell that from your voice." Cook poured tea and sat down next to me at the massive table.

"I'm from Virginia. I am Jenny Habledean Pritcher. My Grandfather, who is with me, is Colonel Benjamin Pritcher. But Clara says he's really a General. We've come to England to find my Uncle Benjamin, who ran away from Mariglenn when he was a boy because Grandfather was angry and told him to go away and never come back. But Grandfather didn't really mean it. Grandfather is very sorry Benjamin left and we all want him to come home. Grandfather and I and Hannah and Mr. Green and Walter and everyone, except Mother, perhaps, who doesn't understand because of her bad nerves."

"Is all this true, child? You've just come to look for Benjamin?"

"Well, no. I've also come to find my cousins because Sophia and Randolf cannot have children because of the Yankees."

"Oh, yes. The American war. And Sophia is your aunt then?"

Yes. She is Mother's sister who lives in Staunton."

"And Staunton is in America, too, then?"

"Yes. It is a real town."

"I can't imagine you'd be making all this up, Missy."

"And also, our cook ran off to be married more than a year ago and our kitchen smelled like this before she left."

"Yes, Missy?"

"Well, perhaps if that man frightens you as he does me, you might want to leave here and come to Mariglenn and be our cook. When we find Benjamin and my cousins we will sail with them back to America on Grandfather's ship. Do you know where my Uncle Benjamin is?"

"No, Jenny, I do not know where your Uncle Benjamin is."

Cook looked about the kitchen. She got up and paced back and forth holding her teacup in both hands. I could see she was thinking, or perhaps praying.

"You say Benjamin left America when he was just a young man?"

"He was just a boy no older than Oliver. Just a little older than me.

"Yes, Miss. That rings true to me now. I was here when Master Benjamin first came here. I was one of the cook's helpers. I love to cook and quite good I am. Fallbright was a grand place then, not wanting a bit for staff. The former Master Pritcher was a fine gentleman and a lighted soul he was. He took your Uncle Benjamin in. Not on account of them having both the Pritcher name, for I don't think Master Pritcher believed Benjamin was a Pritcher. But it didn't matter. It was clear the boy just wanted to belong somewhere. He was as faithful as a sheepdog, he was, and a love for hard work. Master Pritcher had no children then, and his dear lady fretted about it so. They thought young Benjamin was sent straight down from Heaven, they did. Well not a year after your Uncle Benjamin arrived did Lady Pritcher have a son, christened him Wesley after his father, and praised God for him. They said he was a gift from God to them for opening their hearts to young Benjamin."

"Where is Wesley now?" asked Jenny.

"Master Wesley is up in the study as drunk as a Greek sailor, stewing in his jealousy. He's turned Fallbright Hall to a house of pain, he has. Trying to drag everything down with him. I'm sorry, child, you mustn't think I'm bitter. It's just a terrible thing when something good is wasted.

"Young Wesley was always spoiled and hateful. Not that Lady and Master Pritcher spoiled him, mind you. Some say it was his Nanna that filled his head with nonsense she called propriety. She didn't help the lad, but still I could see a dark heart from the day he took his first step. But he and your Uncle Benjamin were like night and day, they were. That made it all the worse. Jealousy choked Wesley. He couldn't bear to hear Benjamin praised, and praised often, Ben was, for he was praiseworthy in all he did, and what a gift for business. Master Pritcher turned over the management of Fallbright to Benjamin before Ben was twenty-one. We prospered then, we did, even in hard times. This house was a house of order and merry production, it was. For your uncle had such a way with people. We all loved him. All of us except Wesley. And Benjamin's wife was like my own daughter, and she'll say so herself, and Katie and Andrew I doted on like they were my own grandchildren."

"Who are Katie and Andrew?"

"Why they're your cousins, dearie. I thought you knew about them. You've talked about little else but cousins since I found you in the hall."

Just then the back door opened and Catherine brought in Grandfather.

"My goodness!" said Cook. "Even soaking wet I can see who you are. Like Adam and Seth, sir, your son is the image of you."

Grandfather came over and took my hands.

"You're alright, then?"

"Yes, because of Cook."

"And I am also safe because of the gallant Mr. Wells. Who I must thank for sending help?"

"This is Cook, and she is like a grandmother to Katie and Andrew, my cousins."

"Yes . . . Yes. I've heard the wonderful news from Mr. Wells. God bless you, Madam."

Grandfather looked about the kitchen. He breathed in deeply.

"The loveliest room in the house, I imagine."

"The only one with a bit of peace, I'll say," answered Cook.

"Catherine, sweetheart. Now hurry off and get Colonel Pritcher some dry towels and be sure not to disturb Master Wesley."

"Yes, Mum."

"Well now, Colonel, it seems that your little Jenny and I have straightened things out. I see there is only one question remaining."

Grandfather looked surprised. "What would that be?" he asked.

"Is the position of cook still available at your estate in Virginia?"

"Very available indeed, Madam."

"And would you consider me for the position?"

Grandfather looked again around the cozy room. He breathed it in.

"You would leave your home and family?"

"Dear Sir, the only real family I've ever had is your son Benjamin and his family. And now that they're gone, Fallbright is no longer home for me."

"See, Grandfather. I do have cousins. Katie and Andrew."

"And a lovely daughter-in-law you have as well, Sir. Her name is Anna Grace, but we call her Gracey. But they're gone now, and

43

they've taken my heart. I'll help you find them, Colonel, and go with you all to America, if you'll have me."

That look came upon Grandfather's face. I knew that he would love to have Cook come and be our cook, but he was going to have his fun.

"I think Jenny and I should have some examples of your craft, Madam, before we decide."

"Craft indeed, Sir? You must be accustomed to rough fare. You may sample my art in a few hours when you've dried off and rested. Catherine, show Colonel Pritcher and Jenny to Benjamin and Gracey's old rooms. See that they have whatever they need. I'll ring when supper is prepared. We'll eat in the kitchen to avoid waking our pickled Master. I intend to be gone from Fallbright before he awakes."

"With pleasure, Mum." Catherine led Grandfather and I up a narrow staircase that led from the kitchen to the upper floors of the great stone manor. The storm had passed and the house was cold and silent. We walked down a long hall where tapestries lined the stone walls. In the wavering light of Catherine's lamp I could see unicorns and peacocks, huntsmen in a green wood, and ladies with long trail dresses and pointed hats.

Catherine opened a heavy wooden door and whispered for us to come in. She went about and lit the lamps and reminded us to be very quiet. She then left us, promising to return soon with towels, hot water and refreshments.

While she was gone, Grandfather and I explored the rooms and told each other what had happened since we were separated in front of the house.

Mr. Wiggle's carriage horse had run wildly down a lane that went by the stables and past many stone walled pastures. Grandfather let him run himself out, then walked him back. He was met by Mr. Wells as he neared the stables.

I told Grandfather what I had learned from Cook, and how she rescued me from Wesley.

Catherine returned, stepping without a sound into the room. She looked about Clara's age and had a round, happy face. She brought hot water and tea, fresh towels, and a special hot drink for Grandfather. She also brought my umbrella and told me that Mr. Wells had found it in the boxwoods.

I told her I could see nothing in the rooms that would tell me anything about my cousins and aunt and uncle. There were no paintings or books or little things that tell you something. Catherine told us that Wesley had everything burned that Benjamin and Gracey didn't take with them.

"And they took very little, for Wesley chased them out with scarcely a few hours to prepare. That was more than a year ago. Master Benjamin hardly raised a complaint, only saying he wouldn't stay where he wasn't wanted. Nearly all the staff offered to go with him though he forbid them and told them he wouldn't have his friends homeless on his account, for he had no place to go and no opportunity on account of all the letters Wesley had written. He told us that being homeless was more lonely than we knew."

Grandfather excused himself and walked to a dark corner of another room. I saw his eyes glistening as he left.

"I'm sorry, Colonel Pritcher. Cook says I do prattle on without thinking, and she's right."

Grandfather's voice came unsteady from the dark corner. "Does anyone have any idea where my son and his family are?"

"I don't know, Colonel, Sir. I don't think Master Benjamin knew where he was going when he left. There was no time to plan. Wesley was in such a drunken rage and Gracey feared for the children. Though Mr. Wells knows Benjamin better than anyone and I think he would have the best guess."

"What letters did Wesley write that you spoke of?" Grandfather asked Catherine.

"Letters to the authorities, even advertisements in the London papers, all accusing Benjamin of trying to defraud the estate after Wesley's father's death. Wesley so crafted the lies, mixing them with truths and half-truths that anyone not fully acquainted with the situation would most likely believe his lies. And then Wesley threw Benjamin out. And to see the family, God bless them, walking down the lane away from Fallbright. If you didn't know better, you'd think they were running from something. Wesley planned it that way, out of his miserable hatred. Well, Cook and I and Mr. Wells are all that's left and we've agreed to leave together, without giving Wesley any warning, and taking nothing, mind you, but our own things, for his false accusations would follow us too, like bloodhounds. We want to leave tonight after supper with you and Jenny, if you'll allow us,

Sir. We'll help you find Benjamin if we can."

Grandfather came back into the room. He was strong now. "We will find them. And all of you are welcome to come with us if you like," he said.

After dinner, Grandfather pushed his plate back from the kitchen table.

"What is your real name, Madam?" he asked Cook.

"Cook is my name, Victoria Cook. Born with the name made me believe food was my destiny."

"Indeed, Mrs. Cook. I would be irresponsible to keep you from your destiny. I believe the veal with mint jelly, or perhaps it was the dill bread and asparagus soup, has convinced me that my destiny is to enjoy you fulfilling your destiny."

I helped clean up the dishes to show I was not spoiled. Everything was settled before we were through. Cook was coming to Mariglenn to be our cook and to keep on being like a grandmother to Katie and Andrew, and like a mother to Benjamin and Gracey, once we found them. For I knew we would find them and even Grandfather now believed we would find them.

While I was helping Cook and Catherine clean up and get their things together, Grandfather went out to the stables with Mr. Wells to ready the carriage. Catherine and I tiptoed through the large house putting out the few lamps that remained. We passed the study where Wesley still slumped in his chair. The fire in his hearth was out, and he muttered in his sleep. The candle on his stand was burned to a nub and flickering. Perhaps it was a draft down the chimney or the rustle of our skirts as we passed, but before we reached the stairs his light went out and we left him alone in the darkness.

On to Scotland

We found Mr. Wiggle back at the pub. He was still refreshing himself and singing very loudly. Everyone thanked us for taking him out. Grandfather and Mr. Wells sat him in the back of the carriage and tied him on top of the luggage.

Mrs. Cook and Catherine and Mr. Wells were eager to be far away from Fallbright before morning, so we all crowded in the carriage and rode through the night toward Bristol. Mr. Wiggle sang the whole way, and the bumping and shaking of the carriage gave his singing a funny sound so that everyone was laughing, which I think encouraged Wiggle to keep singing.

I must have fallen asleep somewhere, for the next thing I recall is waking up on a train. I was in a little compartment with Cook and Catherine. Grandfather and Mr. Wells were in another compartment across the hall. When I awoke, Cook was setting out tea and cakes and sent Catherine to get Grandfather and Mr. Wells. Then we all had tea together. We were all tired and not as cleaned up as we would have liked, but everyone was happy.

I asked Grandfather where we were going. Grandfather said that Mr. Wells would explain, so everyone hushed and looked at Mr. Wells.

"I've been thinking on this ever since Ben and the family were put out, for I always planned to follow him. I knew I had to find 'em in my mind, for Ben was not to leave a trail. He worried for his family and what would become of them because of Wesley's twisted mischief, and didn't want to chance his friends suffering as well.

"Now we know that Ben had not much money of his own to speak of, because Wesley tricked him out of what was in his accounts in London just weeks before putting him out. And we know he's too rightly proud to go changing his name, and too smart to try and save his good name in the face of what Wesley had done. Now we also know that Gracey was an orphan, though perhaps the most lovely orphan that ever lived, and has no family that we know of. So under the circumstances, there's only one place on earth they could've gone. Where any of us would go if all of proper England had given us the boot."

"Where is that?" I asked.

"To Scotland, of course, little miss."

I did not understand Mr. Wells, but it seemed to make sense to everyone else. Grandfather raised his teacup and made a toast.

"To Scotland, then."

"To find my cousins," I said. "Hurray for Scotland."

Everyone cheered, "Hurray for Scotland and cousins," and lots of tea was spilled but nobody minded because it was a grand adventure and we were friends.

Our journey to Scotland was filled with train stations and meals in the dining car, trying to freshen up without a proper bath, and telling stories.

I told the story about being rescued by Oliver in the snowstorm and all about my magic desk and chair.

Grandfather told about Virginia and the Allegheny Mountains. About growing up at Mariglenn and what it was like before the war. But he said nothing about what happened in the war. Grandfather also told about other countries and tropical islands and about people I had never heard of before. Grandfather seemed happier than I ever remembered and talked more than ever, too.

Cook and Catherine told me all about my cousins so I would know things about them when we found them in Scotland.

They said that Andrew is fifteen and very grown up. That he loved to read and write like me and had a good head for numbers, too. How he could ride a horse and drive a carriage and loved to tinker about in the smithy shop and fancied himself an inventor. Cook said he was quick to mind his father and that he honored his mother like she was The Queen herself.

They told me that Katie was only six and the shyest creature on earth. That she hardly spoke to anyone outside the family, for she was the only little girl at Fallbright.

They all worried the most for Katie, for though Andrew might consider being put out into the world a wonderful adventure, Katie was very frightened to have things turned upside down.

I told everyone that I would take care of Katie. That she could be my sister and my cousin. I said that Grandfather had given me a brass key with a green tassel, that it was a key to the best things in all the world and that I would share everything with Katie, and that no one would ever make Katie go away from Mariglenn or make her afraid.

I told them that my Hannah was waiting at home for us and already knew that I was bringing home cousins and was ready to love them up.

Grandfather explained about Mother's bad nerves, and about what some people in Virginia thought about Yankees and losing the war. He told them about Mr. Marlowe and the woodshop and other things I already knew about.

We stopped in many towns and cities but the stations looked much the same. Then I saw the green hills. Hills without trees, as if the Allegheny Mountains had lost their clothes. Hills with sheep and stone fences, and some hills with just sheep.

Mr. Wells told me we were in Scotland. I thought it was like Virginia, but sleepier.

We asked at every station if anyone had seen Benjamin and his family, but no one could remember. I wondered if they came to Scotland in a train or a carriage or if they walked all the way. Mr. Wells seemed certain they would have come by train. He said though Benjamin did not have the money that was rightfully his, he did have a bit of something and it was certainly enough for train fare and some extra to boot. I prayed that God would watch over them. I prayed they would not be hungry or cold. I prayed most of all that we would find them soon.

We got off the train in the city of Edinburgh, where Grandfather took us to a nice hotel.

We all had a hot bath, then met together in the dining room. As we ate we talked about how we might find Benjamin and his family. But how would we know where they were, I wondered. Edinburgh was a big city, but just a little dot on the map of Scotland. I was beginning to worry we might not find them.

After dinner I was very tired and Catherine took me up to bed. We said our prayers together. We prayed that God would show us where to find Benjamin and his family. I told Catherine about mustard seed faith. She said she believed in faith, too, and that we should put our little mustard seeds together.

That night I had a dream. I dreamed I saw Katie and though I had never seen her before, I just knew it was her.

In the dream, Katie was sitting on a beautiful little pony on the edge of a cliff overlooking the sea. Her long brown hair was tossing all about in the wind and mixing with her pony's brown, shaggy mane. Together they looked out to sea where there were many tiny islands. I called out to her, but she did not hear me. I called to her pony and told him to take good care of Katie until I came to take her home to Mariglenn. The pony heard and understood, for he stomped the ground and nodded his head.

At breakfast the next morning I told everyone my dream. Mr. Wells became very excited.

"The Shetland Islands, Missy. You've seen a bloomin' vision of the Shetlands."

Mr. Wells told me the Shetland Islands were a group of small islands about one hundred miles northeast of the Scottish mainland. Mrs. Cook spread a map on the table and showed me.

"How can we get there?" I asked.

Grandfather said he would send word back to Liverpool for Captain Johnson to bring the *St. Anna* up the coast to the Firth of Clyde, then up the Clyde River to Glasgow where we would meet them. Grandfather said he would also have Captain Johnson send word to Clara in Cumbria to meet us in Glasgow. Then we would all sail together to the Shetland Islands.

After breakfast Grandfather and I went to the telegraph station to send our messages. I watched as the telegraph man tapped on the machine. The noises that it made did not sound like messages at all, but the man explained that the sounds were a special code that another telegraph man could understand.

We sent a message for Captain Johnson in Liverpool and also one for the hotel in London to have our baggage sent immediately to our ship.

After we sent our messages, Grandfather and I walked slowly back to the hotel together.

Flowers bloomed everywhere, for everyone in the city had a little garden. Even the shopkeepers grew flowers in window boxes. The flowers looked so gay and bright against the gray stone of buildings and the blue blanket of sky.

Glasgow was a dingy city like Bristol. There were factories that spewed out sooty smoke, and many broken down buildings. The rough people looked so tired and sad and the well-dressed people pretended not to see them.

From my room in the hotel I could see the river. The docks were crowded with ships and men hauling bundles and pushing carts.

I don't know why, but watching the busy waterfront made me afraid. Afraid that believing I would find my cousins was a silly thing.

Maybe I had a dream about Katie because I wanted to see her so bad that my heart made up the dream. I worried that Grandfather and Mr. Wells would be disappointed with me if we did not find Benjamin on the Shetland Islands. I told Catherine and Cook my feelings. Cook said it was the spirit of the city that troubled me and not to pay it any mind. Catherine told me she felt the same feeling. She said she had the strangest thought that the people of the city were loading up all their hope and kindness onto the boats, then watching it sail away.

I asked Catherine if she wanted to come with us and live at Mariglenn. She said she would love to, but was not yet sure that she should but felt she would know soon enough.

Mustard Seeds

I was so happy to be back on board the *St. Anna*. The cozy cabin was waiting for me. My things had been neatly put away and my writing book was on the little table with fresh flowers and a small box of treats. Before I could even wonder who had arranged things so, Clara jumped through the doorway and said, "Boo!"

Clara hugged and kissed me and laughed.

She told me she had only stayed three days in Cumbria because her friend became very sick. She had to come back to Liverpool, which was dreadfully boring because she had no escort and had to spend most of her time at the hotel.

I told her all that had happened since we parted. She thought it was wonderful we were following my dream to the Shetland Islands, as she had never been there. She said perhaps we should not tell her father that we were sailing to the Shetlands on account of a little girl's dream, for Captain Johnson did not believe in such things. Clara believed. She said she often had dreams which came true. Maybe only little unimportant things, yet they came true all the same.

Clara and I would share the cabin and Catherine and Mrs. Cook shared another cabin next to ours. Grandfather roomed with Captain Johnson.

Cook and Catherine and Clara and I made a place in my cabin for Katie. I gave Catherine two of my best dresses to alter to Katie's size. We put together a little box of special things Katie would need. We did this to show we believed. We called ourselves the Mustard Seed Ladies.

Three days after the *St. Anna* arrived in Glasgow we set sail for the Shetland Islands. The voyage took us southwest to the mouth of Clyde Firth, then northward up the Scottish coast between the Inner and Outer Hebrides, then northeast past the Orkney Islands and on to the Shetlands.

In four days we reached the islands and anchored in the harbor at Scalloway. I went ashore with Grandfather and Mr. Wells in the skiff to find the constable in Scalloway, and ask him if he had heard of a Pritcher family having come to the islands recently. The constable had not heard of anyone named Pritcher, but said he'd seen a new chap and his son at a pony auction in Lerwick two weeks past. He said he wasn't one of the regular pony buyers that come from the mainland and that they didn't look a bit Scottish. He told us we'd likely find out more in Lerwick.

Lerwick was only a few miles away, so we hired a carriage to take us. We stopped at the first pub we saw, as Mr. Wiggle had taught us to do. I stayed with Grandfather in the carriage while Mr. Wells went inside. We waited in the wind and the warm sun, watching the grass on the treeless hills flutter, changing from green to golden gray. Then it happened.

Something strange and beautiful came over me. At first it frightened me, for I had never felt anything like it before. I grabbed Grandfather's arm and nearly screamed that we should return to the ship at once. Grandfather looked at me a little sternly for a moment, then he must have felt it as well. He quickly fetched Mr. Wells and told him we were returning to the ship.

We did not speak the whole way. I was letting the strange feeling guide me, and as I did I lost all fear. I knew where they were. I knew where Katie was. All my feelings were burning like a brightness that was not hot but warm and excited. We were back on the ship. I asked Grandfather if we could set sail and if he would allow me to guide the ship. He did not answer, but went away to speak with Captain Johnson. I stayed alone on the deck in the sun and wind, trying to protect the beautiful feeling. Grandfather returned with the Captain, who was huffing and making a protest, saying he thought it unwise and improper for me to pilot a sailing vessel. Grandfather took Captain Johnson away privately then returned in a moment with the first mate. Grandfather told me that we would set sail immediately, that the first mate would man the wheel and that I should show him where to sail the ship.

I sat atop a large barrel next to Mr. McWallind, who was the first mate. Grandfather and the Captain stood to his other side. Only minutes before the winds were contrary, but had now shifted. The sails fluttered then snapped taut. The bright feeling filled me again and I stretched out my hand and pointed the way.

Return to Mariglenn

We sailed out of the harbor and into the North Sea. Then I pointed south down the coast of the main island. We passed between the small islands. Grassy cliffs towered above our sails. Then I saw Katie. First only a hazelnut dot on the distant cliff's edge. I pointed until Grandfather could see her too. Her pony stomped and shuffled in the wind. I jumped off the barrel and ran to the rail and waved my hand to Katie. The ship turned toward the little island to search for a harbor. Katie finally saw me waving on the deck and waved back to me. Then the ship rounded a point and we lost sight of each other.

Catherine and Cook and Clara and everyone were now on the deck of the ship. The feeling had filled me so as I could not speak. I just clung to the rail as the anchor was lowered. Grandfather and I and two of the crew set down in the skiff and rowed toward the little dock.

When we were ashore I ran ahead of Grandfather up the hill and toward the cottage. I saw no one, but called out for Benjamin. The cottage door opened and a man who looked like Grandfather only younger came outside. A beautiful lady with hair the color of winter wheat followed him. Katie galloped her pony toward the cottage from where she had been watching at the cliff.

"Uncle Benjamin!" I screamed. "Uncle Benjamin!"

His face was confused as he saw me running toward him. He looked past me to where Grandfather crested the hill. I stopped running. I stood still and looked back at Grandfather looking at Benjamin. Grandfather looked as if he were hurting badly. He fell down on his knees trying to catch his breath but did not take his eyes off Benjamin. He tried to speak but there was no voice. I thought Grandfather was going to die.

What happened next was like a dream. I could no longer hear the sound of the world or see the grass or the sky. I only saw Grandfather crouching in pain. Then appeared a man in a gray uniform. His feet did not touch the ground. I knew who he was. He lifted Grandfather to his feet and smiled at me and spoke to me in my heart, but not in my ears. I cannot write what he told me because it cannot be written. His uniform turned into sunlight. Then he was gone.

Grandfather did not die. He walked on. He passed by me and on to Benjamin. I was still wrapped in the brilliant silence. I saw Andrew there beside Katie and her pony, and Grandfather standing before Benjamin. Grandfather reached out his hand to Benjamin and spoke but I could not hear. Then Benjamin spoke and I heard. He said, "Father, Father, welcome, Father."

The sounds of the world came back. The wind and the sound of the sea. Grandfather hugged Benjamin and Gracey together and I ran to them. Benjamin opened his arms for me and took me up. I told them all I was Jenny Habledean Pritcher. I told them that my father, Nehemiah, died on a hill in Pennsylvania in the war, but it would be alright now. I told Katie and Andrew that their Nanna Cook was waiting on our ship and so was Mr. Wells and Catherine.

Return to Mariglenn

18 June 1867

We are all together. Sailing home on the *Allegheny Princess*, which is the new name for the *St. Anna*. Even Captain Johnson now believes, and he sometimes lets Katie and I take the wheel and steer the ship. When we do, Grandfather closes his eyes and says he fears we will crash or run aground. We tell Grandfather to go below if he is so afraid, but he stays on deck and bellows frightfully. We have on board Katie's little pony and five other beautiful Shetland ponies that Benjamin is bringing to Mariglenn to breed.

That is why Benjamin went to the Shetland Islands. He spent all the money he had to buy the ponies and the cottage farm on the little island.

Mr. Wells has stayed on the Shetland Islands. He is going to buy the best ponies at the sales in Lerwick and bring them to the little island. Each year the *Allegheny Princess* will sail there and bring back some new ponies to America to be sold, and some will come to Mariglenn for Katie and I to take care of.

Mr. Wells is old like Grandfather so Catherine would not let him stay alone. She said she would stay to take care of Mr. Wells and help with the ponies.

Clara says Catherine is in love with a man from Bristol and that Catherine hopes he will marry her and move to the Shetland Islands.

Grandfather bought a small sailing boat in Scalloway for Mr. Wells and Catherine so they could visit the main island and ferry the ponies.

We stayed in the harbor at Scalloway for a week so Captain Johnson could teach Mr. Wells to sail the boat. The crew of the *Allegheny Princess* had a wonderful time watching Mr. Wells learn. When we set sail for home at week's end, Captain Johnson said he would pray for all the ponies that had to sail with Mr. Wells.

20 June 1867

I have decided not to write in my book again until we are all back at Mariglenn. Katie and I and Andrew are very busy taking care of the ponies and telling stories and learning about how to guide the ship by the stars.

Andrew loves the ship and Mr. McWallind says that he has a good hand for the ropes. He climbs about the rigging like a monkey and has already poked about in every corner and cranny.

Uncle Benjamin and Aunty Gracey have given me my own pony. I think she eats too much because she is rounder in the girth than the rest. Katie's pony is named Breezy, for Katie says he gallops like the wind. My pony is skewbald and the color of butterscotch grass against the snow. I have named her Mustard Seed.

Last night I told Katie and Andrew all about the green tasseled key. We were lying in the net of ropes which is slung from the bow of the ship over the water. I said I was not quite sure what the key opened, but it had to do with what Mr. Marlowe was making in the wood shop and that it must be wonderful.

We rose and fell with the sea and watched for falling stars. Katie was afraid to be hanging over the water in the ropes, so I sang her a song that my Hannah sang to me when I was afraid.

The mountains are resting,
The trees close their eyes,
The moon and the stars
Are asleep in the skies.

So hush, Jenny Sweetness,
Hush, Jenny Bell,
Your Hannah will hold you,
And all will be well.

The streams are all falling
From the springs on the hill,
So fall, little Jenny,
Fast asleep and be still.

So hush, Katie Sweetness,
Hush, Katie Bell,
Your Jenny will hold you
And all will be well.

The Highlands

28 July 1867

We are all back at Mariglenn. Everyone is here except Mother, who has been riding trains all around the country with Aunt Sophia. Uncle Randolf passed away soon after we left for England, and Hannah says he has gone to Heaven to be with Father.

Hannah told Benjamin she should give him a whooping for running off and worrying her all these years, but maybe will not whoop him because he has brought back Gracey and Katie and Andrew. Then Hannah changes her mind and says she will whoop Benjamin because she did not get to love on Andrew and Katie when they were little babies. We do not know for sure if Hannah will whoop Benjamin or not, for she cannot make up her mind. Benjamin is silly like Grandfather, and sometimes goes about the house with a feather pillow tied about his backside, saying that he is fearful of Hannah.

Mrs. Cook has already set to work reordering the kitchen. Mr. Green and Hannah say that Mrs. Cook is the best present Grandfather has ever brought them, and Walter especially is careful to please her. Cook spends all morning in the little garden just outside the kitchen. She has planted many seeds she brought from England. They are secret spices and herbs that Cook uses. Grandfather is building an indoor winter garden, all of glass. It will have a fountain fed by the spring on the mountain. Everyone agrees that Cook can have whatever she likes.

Every evening the whole house is excited to know what will be for supper, but Cook lets no one know until it is served.

Grandfather says all his businesses will fail, for he will not leave home to tend to any of them for fear of the meals he will miss.

3 August 1867

Today Walter and Andrew had to cut the doors low on some of the stables so the ponies can hang their heads over when they are inside.

Mr. Marlowe is building a special carriage for Breezy and

Mustard Seed, but says I may not ride Mustard Seed until the carriage is finished. He says it will be a fine riding carriage, only smaller.

Grandfather says if Katie and I are going to ride about the country in our carriage that the roads will never again be safe. He tells Mr. Marlowe to put two brakes on each of our wheels. He also tells us that we must always carry a big horn in the carriage and blow it loudly so other drivers will know to stay clear.

Katie is not yet sure about Grandfather, so I must tell her when we are not to pay him any attention.

10 August 1867

This morning we had a grand surprise. Katie and I went to the stables to see the ponies. Walter told us there was a puppy dog in the paddock with Mustard Seed who would not leave her alone. Katie and I went to see. It was not a puppy but a tiny colt.

We screamed for everyone to come see Mustard Seed's new colt.

Benjamin and Grandfather and Mr. Green all came to see. They said it was not a Shetland colt, that Walter was right, it was a little dog.

Andrew just laughed and carried the colt up to the house to show Gracey and Hannah and Cook and to ask them if they thought it were a puppy or a pony. Everyone said they could not be sure and Hannah even said it might be a baby hyena. Grandfather declared that everyone should pretend it was a pony since Mustard Seed had taken to it, and so as not to upset me and Katie.

But Katie and I know it is Mustard Seed's colt. He follows her everywhere and sucks her milk. We believe that Breezy is the father, for the colt is dark brown like Breezy. Katie and I asked Mustard Seed if we could name her colt Hazelnut. Mustard Seed tells us that Hazelnut is just the name she was thinking of.

13 August 1867

Today Oliver came to take measurements of Breezy and Mustard Seed for their new carriage harness. I introduced him to Andrew and Katie.

Andrew was very polite to Oliver and did not puff up as most boys do. He told Oliver he was eager to have a friend in Virginia. Oliver invited Andrew to go raccoon hunting in the middle of the night with lanterns and noisy dogs. Andrew is delighted to go. Katie and I think it is a very silly thing to do, but we will not say so to the boys. I would like to go into the mountains at night with a light to try and spy a fawn in a thicket or see where the wild turkeys roost. Katie says in England there is a wood where the animals gather at night for a dance and wear clothes like ladies and gentlemen. She read about it in a picture book.

I asked Uncle Benjamin if English animals danced and wore clothes at night. He said they most certainly did and that he shouldn't wonder if animals in Virginia did the same. Hannah says she does not know if Virginia animals would dance as properly as English animals, but said she would sew up clothes for Breezy and Mustard Seed so they would not be shamed if they were invited to a dance.

Katie is very excited about Breezy and Mustard Seed having clothes for a dance and will not let Hannah forget. Hannah asked Katie if our ponies wouldn't settle for just straw hats, but Katie says that will not do.

15 August 1867

It is late at night. I cannot sleep for I can hear the hounds balooing in the mountains.

Andrew wants a raccoon hat and Oliver promises he shall have one. Andrew is reading a book about a man who passed through Hot Springs many years ago and went to live on the Ohio frontier near the Indians. Now Andrew wants to be a mountain man. Oliver says he will teach Andrew all about the mountains and how to live off the land.

Boys are very peculiar. There is something about them that makes me want to be with them, but when I am with them I cannot understand why I want to be with them. Perhaps Andrew and Oliver feel the same, for they are very polite to me but always seem anxious to run off into the mountains or down to the river.

Katie is asleep in my bed. She has her own bed but she cannot sleep unless I hold her and sing a song or tell a story.

My stories are very interesting. I enjoy them myself for I never know what I will say next. Sometimes I think it is not me telling the stories at all, but someone else.

Tonight I told a story about a little girl who was lost in the mountains. A kind raccoon found her and led her to a cave where other friendly animals hide from dogs and boys and have tea together.

Katie interrupted my story to ask if the animals could have a dance, but I went on to explain that all the dances had to be canceled because of so many boys and dogs running about in the mountains.

Katie thought they might have a little dance in the cave, but I said that the cave was small and if they danced and jumped about they would bump their heads on the ceiling.

I could see that Katie was not altogether pleased with the story, so I finished by telling her that the squirrels invited all the animals up to the treetops where they danced under a crescent moon and laughed at the boys and the barking dogs down below.

This made Katie happy and she went right to sleep.

20 August 1867

Mr. Marlowe is going to marry Melinda Taylor and adopt Oliver as his own son. Mr. Marlowe would adopt Jonathan too, but Jonathan ran away. He told the other boys in town he could make his own way in the world and did not need a father. He says he will go out west and find lots of gold.

He stole a horse from Grandfather when he left. Melinda is very upset and came to Mariglenn to tell Grandfather she would somehow pay for the horse, but Grandfather tells her that he will not hear of it and that he will make the horse a going away present to Jonathan. Grandfather says that Jonathan might become a rich prospector someday and surprise everyone.

Even though Jonathan was often mean to Oliver, Oliver is very sad about Jonathan running off. He told Andrew that he is worried that something bad will happen to Jonathan.

Melinda and Mr. Marlowe will be married at the end of September. Katie and I will carry flowers and Oliver will give his mother away. Nanna Cook (this is Katie's name for Cook) will prepare all the food and make a tall cake for the wedding supper.

Katie asked Mr. Marlowe if Breezy and Mustard Seed and Hazelnut could come to the wedding. Mr. Marlowe teased and told Katie if they were properly dressed they were welcome to come. But Katie did not think Mr. Marlowe teased, for she has not let Hannah rest, worrying her about making suits for the ponies.

Now Grandfather is determined to hold everyone to their word and has bought cloth and buttons and lace and tells Hannah she cannot disappoint Katie. Hannah has given in. She says that if Walter can go about in clothes, she sees no reason why the ponies should run around naked.

22 August 1867

Mr. Marlowe has finished the pony carriage. Katie and I have been practicing all day driving around the barn and down the lane. Grandfather hid in the house and only peeked at us from the windows. He finally came out to see. He bit at his fingernails and knocked his knees together, but we did not mind him. We whooshed down the lane, then whooshed up the lane. Breezy and Mustard Seed love to pull the carriage and always run fastest when they're running toward the barn. Hazelnut runs along behind us and whinnies. Even the big horses look up from their grazing to watch us go by.

The carriage has a beautiful green cover with a fringe. The seat is green leather, tufted with red buttons. The spokes on the wheels are painted brightly. One spoke red, the next one black. Black and red, black and red, so that when we whoosh by it looks as though our wheels are the color of coals in the fire.

Aunt Gracey is worried and says that we should only walk the ponies. But Breezy and Mustard Seed do not want to walk. They want to run.

28 August 1867

We had a letter today from Mother and Sophia. They are in San Francisco. Sophia says that Mother is doing well and has not fainted once on the entire trip.

Mother said in the letter that she is greatly enjoying associating with proper society, even Northerners. She says this is a delightful diversion from life in Hot Springs.

I am not sure I understand exactly what Mother means by this, but I'm glad she feels better and has not fainted.

※

29 August 1867

Andrew and Oliver are not to be seen out without their raccoon caps. Nanna Cook and Hannah will not allow the boys to wear the caps in the house for they say they smell and have fleas.

The boys plan to build a cabin in the mountains and camp there through the winter.

Uncle Benjamin and Gracey and Mr. Marlowe and Melinda say they will only allow them if Andrew teaches Oliver to read and write better and work well with numbers. The boys have agreed, and are out in the mountains searching out a good spot for their cabin.

I think Oliver surely wants to be educated. He will learn better from Andrew than from the school master, for Oliver cannot stand to be kept inside.

Katie warns every little animal she sees, telling them that the boys are moving into the woods. She even went to the trout stream and told the fish to swim to the river and tell the other fish to be careful, for Oliver has made fine bamboo fishing rods.

Katie surprises me. She loves to eat fish and venison and rabbit and everything that Nanna Cook prepares. I think Katie has two worlds and she keeps them mostly apart, but there is an in-between place, where her worlds can meet and share.

※

3 September 1867

Grandfather has turned over Mariglenn to Benjamin and Gracey. He says they may run the farm however they wish and can do what they like with the profits. He only requires that they always look after Mother and Hannah and Mr. Green and Walter and Nanna Cook.

Grandfather says he is going to retire from business, but Mr. Green says that is the craziest thing he has ever heard and says it will never happen. But I wonder if Mr. Green understands what

Grandfather means. I overheard Grandfather speaking with Mr. Marlowe in the study last night. I was supposed to be in bed but Katie wanted some warm milk.

I know I should not have listened, but I heard Mr. Marlowe say something about "the project," that it would be finished before the wedding. I knew they spoke of what Mr. Marlowe was working on in the back shop. Grandfather said that after the wedding he would "turn it over to the children." He said he would then retire and never again leave Mariglenn, for he was tired of tromping all over the world. He told Mr. Marlowe that he had given me the green tasseled key and said it was safest in my hands.

Mr. Marlowe asked Grandfather about the rest of the keys. Grandfather told him that he would know concerning them soon enough.

I dared not listen at the study door any longer, so I brought Katie her milk. Then I got out the green tasseled key from the little hidden drawer in my desk. I told Katie a story about the key and it was such a good story that I've written it down.

The Lost Stories

Key and Tassel

How the Key Got His Emerald Green Tassel
By Jenny Habbledean Pritcher

Long ago the world was divided in half by a Great Stone Wall. On one side of the Wall there were Clocks and Bowls and Spoons and Saddles and Candles and Dresses and Sewing Needles and all sorts of Things living in the land, but there were no People and no Animals.

The People and Animals lived on the other side of the Wall and believed that the Great Stone Wall was the end of the world. The Things believed that the Great Stone Wall was just another Thing, only a very big Thing. The King of the Land of Things was a magnificent mahogany Chest of Drawers. He was as tall as the Grandfather Clock, but had broad shoulders and claw feet and flaming finials upon his crown.

The Queen was a lovely Silk Gown embroidered with gold and trimmed in royal blue satin.

One day the King and Queen gave a party. They invited the Books to come and tell stories, the Fiddles and the Flutes and the Drums to make music, the Lamps and the Candles to give their light, and all the other Things were invited to come and do whatever they did best. The Grandfather Clock was invited so he could tell everyone when it was time to go home at the end of the party.

Now on the same day when the Things were having their party on one side of the Great Stone Wall, the People and Animals were in big trouble on their side of the wall.

You see, the King of the People and the Animals was a grave old School Master. And on the day before, most of the People and Animals were hooting and hollering and making a fuss, and running around with no clothes on, for of course they had no clothes.

Well, King School Master was very displeased, so he ordered that on the next day, everyone must sit down and be quiet all day long.

So while the People and Animals were sitting sadly being very quiet, the Things were having their party. Now the Things happened to be having a very fun and very loud party.

The Pots and Pans were jumping up and down on the Tables while the Instruments were singing and the Books were reading as loudly as they could to be heard above the other Things. The Carriages were playing hide and seek with the Furniture out in the Royal Stables and knocking into the Buckets and the Tools.

The King and Queen let it all go and said they would let everyone enjoy themselves and the Mops and Brooms could just clean up the mess in the morning.

The only ones behaving themselves were a little Brass Key and a fine White Candle, who were in the Royal Library talking softly about the Paintings and the Tapestries and wondering wonderful things like what made Knives so sharp and Rugs so flat and Spinning Wheels so spindly. The Key graciously wondered aloud why the flame of the Candle was so beautifully bright. The Candle, who was sitting primly in her Candle Holder, blushed and wondered back why the Key fit so perfectly in his Lock and could free it open with hardly any effort, yet no one else could do it at all.

Meanwhile the People and the Animals on the other side of the Wall were sitting perfectly quiet. Now the King had also ordered that during this day of silence that everyone should think about how bad they had been the day before and what they would do to keep such a ruckus from happening ever again.

But no one was really thinking about that. They were only pretending to think about yesterday's badness.

Some were thinking about what mischief they could get into tomorrow, especially the Boys and the Dogs and the Monkeys.

Some were thinking about how to make the world happier and more cheerful. These were the Girls and the Ponies and the Hummingbirds and Little Fawns.

Some, like the Grandpas and the Black Bears and the Elephants were thinking nothing at all but had fallen to sleep.

In fact, the old King School Master had fallen asleep himself and was making funny noises with his nose.

Now also in the land was a little Yellow Finch. She had fluttered over to the far side of the Kingdom where she could be quiet by herself. And while she was being quiet and thinking about the sky and the wind and the sunshine, she thought she heard some very funny noises. She thought she heard bumping and clattering and tooting and hooting and smashing and scuffling and yes, she could even hear singing a far ways off.

So the Yellow Finch jumped from her perch and flew toward the noises. Farther and farther and higher and higher she flew until she disappeared in the clouds. Then suddenly, the clouds parted and she saw that she had flown right over the Wall that was the end of the world. But it was not the end of the world. For there was grass and hills and rivers and trees, just like in her world. So she flew on to explore the new world and to learn where the strange noises were coming from.

Soon she saw the Castle, so she flew down and perched in a tree in the courtyard. And what she saw was hard for her to believe. She saw Kettles boiling over and Wagon Wheels chasing Pin Cushions. She saw Hair Brushes dancing with Flower Vases and Bridles and Saddles and Rocking Chairs in the pond paddling a Flatboat.

Now at this same time, the Candle and the Brass Key were gazing out the Library Window into the Courtyard and happened to see the Yellow Finch. They had never seen such a Thing before and called down to her and asked her name. The Finch was very shy but did not want to be rude, so she flew to the Window Ledge. She introduced herself and told the Candle and the Key where she came from and about the People and Animals on her side of the Wall.

The Key and the Candle were very excited to know what was on the other side of the Wall, for just moments before they were conversing about the Wall and wondering why the Wall stood so cold and tall and never spoke to anyone.

Now the Key and the Candle were eager to see the other world for themselves, so they asked the Yellow Finch if she would fly them back to her world. Certainly the Finch was willing to take them, but did not think she could hold them both in her small talons. The Key solved the problem by asking a little Wicker Basket to go along with them.

The Key and the Candle climbed into the Wicker Basket, who was happy to go along. The Yellow Finch took hold of the Basket's slender handle and out the window she flew. Higher and higher again she rose in the air and back toward the Great Stone Wall.

Now the Yellow Finch had been flying all day and was getting very tired. So when she saw the top of the Wall she alighted there for a rest.

The day was now clear, and from the top of the Wall the four friends could clearly see both of their worlds. Before them they could see the People and the Animals sitting quietly far below.

Behind them they saw the Things enjoying their noisy party. This was an interesting sight and the friends thought for a long time about what they saw.

Finally the little Wicker Basket said that he thought that the Things and the Creatures might get on well together. Well, that was just the same thing the others were thinking. But how will everyone get past the Wall so they might all get together? Just then they were all startled by a deep booming voice.

"They could go through my door."

"Who is that?" the friends all asked at once.

"I am the Great Stone Wall," said the Stone Wall.

"Why have you never told anyone before that there was a door between the worlds?" asked the Candle.

"Because no one ever asked me," said the Wall.

"Where is your door?" asked the Yellow Finch.

"You do not need a door, brave little Finch, for you have wings and can fly above me."

"But," said the Key, "the Creatures and the Things will need your door if they are ever going to get together."

"Do you think it wise for them to get together?" asked the Great Stone Wall.

Now this question caused the friends to be quiet and to think for awhile.

At last the Key broke the silence. "I think everyone should have a chance at getting together."

"Very well," said the Great Stone Wall. "The door is straight down below you near the ground."

So straight down the Yellow Finch flew, carrying her friends. And there was the door just as the Wall had said. But the door was locked shut.

"How will we open this door without a key?" said the Key.

Then all the others gave Key a funny look.

"Oh yes, I nearly forgot myself. I am a key," said Key.

So Key tried himself in the lock. He twisted and pushed then twisted back the other way. He fiddled and wiggled and pried.

"It's no use," said the Key. "I am not the right key."

The Lost Stories

"But you are the only key we have," replied the others at once.

Then the fine white Candle spoke sweetly to the Key. "Try again, only gently this time, dear, and I'm sure you'll open the door."

The Key could not refuse the Candle, so he tried himself in the lock again. He carefully adjusted himself, letting his notches and teeth find their own way. Then he gently twisted. The lock released and the door flung open.

"Hurray! Hurray!" they all shouted. "Now there is a door between the worlds."

So Yellow Finch flew on to tell the People and the Animals that there was an open door at the Great Stone Wall at the end of the world. The Key and Candle and the Wicker Basket ran back to the Castle to tell the King and the Queen and all the other Things about the door in the Great Stone Wall.

The Yellow Finch first landed on King School Master's shoulder. She awoke him from his nap and told him of the door at the end of the world and of the other world beyond the door. The School Master was very upset and told the Yellow Finch to be quiet. But the Yellow Finch was far too excited to be quiet so she flew all about and told everyone about the door at the end of the world.

The Boys and the Dogs and the Monkeys were the first to go running off toward the end of the world. The School Master screamed at them to sit down and be quiet, but they paid him no mind.

The Girls and the Ponies and the Hummingbirds and the Little Fawns slowly made their way toward the Wall as well, for they were curious but did not want to do anything wrong.

The Grandpas and the Bears and the Elephants went right on sleeping.

Back at the Castle of the Things, the news spread quickly about the door in the Great Stone Wall and Everything made a wild dash for the door.

The four friends had gone on ahead and all met together at the door where they waited to see what would happen…. And this is what happened.

The Boys and the Dogs and the Monkeys were the first to reach the door. They ran right through without even slowing down and the first Things they saw were Guns and Jackknives and Tins of Tobacco and Bones and Cannonballs and Dirty Boots and Greasy

Return to Mariglenn

Tools and Matchsticks and they all got on well indeed, and seemed to like each other very much.

Slowly the Girls and the Ponies and the Hummingbirds and the Little Fawns came near the Wall and saw lots of marvelous Things coming through the door.

There were Dresses and Saddles and Sugar Cubes and Books and Writing Desks and Down Pillows and Hair Brushes.

Everything and Everyone got to know each other in time and friendships were made, and from that day on there was a lot of coming and going between the worlds until it was all one world. Even the School Master came around when he was introduced to Chalk and Arithmetic Books and a good stiff Hickory Switch.

And the Yellow Finch built a nest on top of the Wall where she could sit quietly and look down on the worlds.

The Wicker Basket was picked up by a little Girl and used to carry Wildflowers and warm brown Bread.

And the Brass Key was knighted by King Chest of Drawers and given a handsome emerald green tassel by Queen Silk Gown.

The Key and the Candle were then married, and in time they had little Brass Keys for children that shone as brightly as gold.

The End

5 September 1867

Katie is very fond of the story and has fun talking with things in the house.

I read my story at breakfast this morning and everyone enjoyed it, but everyone thought the story had a different meaning.

Nanna Cook says the story explains how her good kitchen knives keep disappearing, along with bottles of wine from the cellar.

Mr. Green says the story teaches that there is a saddle for every bottom and a bottom for every saddle. Though he said this a little differently and was scolded by Hannah.

Grandfather says the story should remind some of us that little yellow finches should not listen in on things that are none of their business.

But I did not mean the story to mean anything, but only to put Katie to sleep.

Mountain Men

6 September 1867

Andrew and Oliver have gone into the mountains today to build their cabin. They've taken one of the older Shetland ponies, whom they call Buckshot, and loaded him down with supplies and tools.

Katie and I asked them where they would build their cabin and they just said somewhere in Mariglenn, which is not saying anything at all because Mariglenn is very big and spreads way up into the western mountains. They will come back for the wedding and then return to their cabin. They say they will stay in the mountains until spring and live like real mountain men. Hannah told them they were starting off well because they already smelled like real mountain men.

Katie and I followed them as far as we could in our carriage. I did not want to tell them at first, but I knew I would miss them both very much. When we reached the edge of the pasture where the forest began, I could not help myself. I climbed down from the carriage and gave both boys a hug and a kiss and told them I loved them. I even gave Buckshot a hug and kissed his black muzzle. I made them promise to be careful and to bathe occasionally. They only promised they would be careful.

I said we must have a picnic together when they returned in the spring, and they could tell us of their adventures in the mountains. They agreed to this and Oliver even said he would write of their adventures in my writing book if I would like, for he was serious about learning to read and write well.

I was happy that Oliver was eager about reading and writing. I think that even mountain men should not be ignorant.

10 September 1867

Hannah has finished making clothes for Breezy and Mustard Seed. She has only made a cap for Hazelnut, saying that Hazelnut is too young for a whole suit.

Walter helped us dress the ponies. He says he is worried now that all the horses will want clothes. He said if Miss Katie had her way he'd spend the rest of his life dressing and undressing every critter on the farm.

Mustard Seed was very willing to put on her new clothes and didn't fuss a bit. She has a pale blue dress with white lace and a matching blue bonnet.

Breezy did not mind his shirt and jacket, but he pitched a fit about his britches. Walter got kicked twice before he finally got them on.

Breezy's shirt is starched white and his jacket and britches are dark blue. He has a stovepipe hat that ties under his chin and a blue neck tie.

Breezy and Mustard Seed make a handsome couple and look very dignified. Hazelnut wears his little wool cap cocked to one side and looks like the mischievous rascal that he is. We hitched the ponies to the carriage and rode right up to the front of the house.

Hannah came out and fussed with the new outfits. She adjusted ties and buttons and smoothed the cloth. She said that Walter could hardly dress himself and had no business dressing fine ponies like Breezy and Mustard Seed.

Katie called for her mother to come and see. Everyone came out to the front drive. They walked around the carriage admiring the ponies. Benjamin tucked Breezy's ears inside his hat and straightened his tie. Grandfather said Breezy's white shirt was one of his own and was surprised it fit Breezy so nicely. Everyone agreed that Breezy and Mustard Seed would fit in properly at any occasion.

Katie was so pleased.

15 September 1867

This evening Buckshot came back to the stables alone. He was still wearing his saddle but his bridle was gone. Andrew and Oliver should come back soon to fetch him. Katie says that Buckshot does not want to be a mountain pony, but would rather be a stable pony who eats good grain and keeps good company.

Maybe that is true, but I am worried about Andrew and Oliver.

Benjamin and Mr. Marlowe say that if the boys do not return by morning to get Buckshot then they will go and find them.

16 September 1867

The boys did not return this morning. Katie and I will go with Benjamin and Mr. Marlowe to find them. We will also bring three of the hunting dogs to help us because they have good noses and can smell where the boys are. Hannah says anyone ought to be able to smell the boys out by now and there was no need to trouble the dogs.

They are not saying so, but I think everyone is worried about Andrew and Oliver. I feel a strange feeling. A feeling I've never had before. I do not know what it means and I cannot imagine why the boys did not come home to get Buckshot.

Katie and I will ride our ponies. Katie understands that finding Andrew and Oliver is important work so Breezy and Mustard Seed cannot wear their outfits.

I'll write about what happens when we return.

17 September 1867

The family has agreed not to tell anyone about what Andrew and Oliver have discovered in the mountains. It's all very strange and wonderful.

Katie even told Breezy and Mustard Seed and the hound dogs not to tell any other animals, but she is worried that the hound dogs cannot keep a secret.

The dogs had no problem finding the boys' camp on a flat overlooking the river about two miles southwest of the house. When we caught up with them we found their shelter and the beginnings of their cabin with their tools and supplies left undisturbed. It looked as if they had just gone for a walk or a swim in the river, but we did not see them anywhere. Mr. Marlowe said their fire pit was cold, so they had probably been gone for some time.

The dogs balooed around the camp for a long time until finally they picked up a scent and headed off into the woods. We followed up the rocky slope.

Up ahead the dogs stopped and were circling about a large beech tree. We soon discovered the reason, for when we reached the tree we found Buckshot's bridle hanging from the lowest limb, the reins tied securely.

The dogs were off again, up the steep mountainside over huge boulders and fallen tree trunks. The horses and ponies could go no further so we tied them off at the beech tree.

We climbed carefully up the mountain, watching out for copperheads and rattlesnakes in rock crevices and under logs. The dogs stopped again on a ledge and howled excitedly.

Katie is a wonderful rock climber and was first to reach the ledge. She called down, saying there was a hole in the rocks, and she could smell smoke.

That is how we found Andrew and Oliver.

The Caverns

In a few minutes the dogs found the main entrance to the caverns where the large stone had been pried aside. Their echoing howls boomed out of the opening as they disappeared down the passage. We found a lantern and some rope near the entrance along with Oliver's hatchet.

Suddenly we heard the boys' voices mixed with the barking of the dogs. The sounds were getting closer and soon Andrew and Oliver appeared at the entrance blinking at the daylight. They were very excited to see us but wondered why we had come to find them, for they did not know that Buckshot had gotten loose and ran back to the stables.

Benjamin told them they looked and smelled like real mountain men. The boys were pleased by that and told us they had found a wonderful place inside the mountain and had been exploring it for some time. They said they were coming out to get more firewood when they heard the dogs coming down the passage.

There was no more kerosene for the lamp, so the boys led us down the passageway by the light of a candle. We had all gathered some firewood and carried it with us. Benjamin and Mr. Marlowe noticed little things about the stone walls and the floor but especially the steps. They talked about the fine tooling and how long it must have taken to complete the spiraled staircase. Katie counted one hundred and twenty steps down until we reached another passage, which soon widened then emptied into a great room. We could see the glowing coals of what was left of the fire. A little shaft of daylight poked through the ceiling high above.

Mr. Marlowe quieted the dogs, for their barking bounced wildly off the walls and spoiled the peace of the underworld hall.

We put a bundle of wood on the coals and soon the vast chamber was lighted by the amber flames.

The boys told us they only explored one other passage and that it led to a huge cavern filled with large baskets neatly lined in rows. They had removed a number of the basket lids and discovered them to be filled with dry bones.

"Look up here," said Benjamin. He reached up to a tiny platform carved in the limestone just above his head at the entrance of the cemetery room and brought down a clay bowl that was obviously a kind of lamp. The wick was as thick as my small finger.

"It's beeswax." Benjamin touched the wick to the flame of Oliver's candle and instantly the greater light filled the cavern.

The ceiling and floor as far as we could see were ever so strange. It looked like the rocks were dripping to the floor and the floor was dripping up to the ceiling. There was yellow and red and orange and white and brown. Water was trickling off the pointy rocks. I don't really have the words to say about what we saw. It was like we were on the inside of the world. In a place that people are not supposed to be, but maybe if they were in trouble and needed to hide they would come to this place.

I cannot write anymore about this because Grandfather has strictly told everyone in the house not to tell anyone about the caverns. There has been a lot of whispering in the house about what Oliver and Andrew discovered in the mountains.

Return to Mariglenn

Wedding Cake

27 September 1867

Mr. Marlowe and Melinda Taylor were married this morning on the lawn at Mariglenn. Mother and Aunt Sophia came home for the wedding and to visit for a few weeks. But when Mother saw Breezy and Mustard Seed and Hazelnut with the other guests, she fainted and had to be carried into the house. Katie thought Mother fainted because Hazelnut wore no clothes except for his woolen cap.

We had a splendid party after the wedding with two giant cakes. Nanna Cook made the second cake for the ponies. Katie and I tasted the ponies' cake but it was not as good as the people's cake.

Mother came out to the lawn for the party but the first thing she saw was Hazelnut eating cake, and even though Katie had put a lovely blue cape on him that went well with his hat, Mother fainted again.

Grandfather says Mother fainted because Hazelnut looked too much like a Yankee officer.

I am worried Mother will not stay at home long.

28 September 1867

Late last night after all the wedding guests were gone and after I had already gone to bed, Hannah woke me and whispered for me to fetch my green tasseled key and come down to the study. When I came down I was surprised to see Mr. Marlowe and Melinda, for I supposed they had already left. Uncle Benjamin and Aunt Gracey were also there with Grandfather and Hannah.

In the corner of the room, to the right of the big fireplace, stood what appeared a magnificent chest of drawers. It had beautiful carvings that looked like spreading fans and finials like flaming torches. I thought for a moment that it was a wedding gift from Grandfather to Mr. Marlowe and Melinda, but thought better of it knowing that Mr. Marlowe was the only one who could make such a fine piece of furniture.

No one in the room spoke a word, but they all looked at me. I thought they were just surprised to see me in my nightclothes, so I excused myself and sat on the sofa with Hannah. Grandfather came and sat next to me and held my hand and Hannah took hold of my other hand.

Grandfather gazed intently at the beautiful piece of furniture. He spoke softly but clearly so everyone could hear. He asked me to take the green tasseled key and go over to the tall chest of drawers. When I had done so he asked me to open the drawer at the middle of the case.

I put the key into the lock and slowly turned. To my surprise the drawer front fell gently forward and laid level, revealing a finely fitted interior. It wasn't a chest of drawers at all, but a lovely secretary desk.

"Do you know what this is?" Grandfather asked.

"Yes," I said. "It's what Mr. Marlowe has been working on in the back shop."

"That's right, Jenny. And do you remember what I told you when we walked together that evening in Alexandria, and what I said when I first gave you the green tasseled key?"

"You said the key was the key to the best things in all the world."

"That is what I said, but you gave the key back and told me you would rather have your cousins than all the best things in the world. Do you still feel that way, Jenny? Would you give up the key for your cousins?"

"I would give up anything for Andrew and Katie."

I walked back to Grandfather and put the green tasseled key into his open hand.

Grandfather looked into my eyes. I could feel his love wrapped around me like a blanket of sunshine. For a moment he did not look old, neither did he look young. I thought he looked as he would appear in Heaven. Grandfather was happy.

"I love you, Jenny."

"I love you, too, Grandfather."

"Hannah, please fetch Mr. Wallace from the parlor."

I was surprised. I recognized the tall gentleman. He had come to the wedding. He was a lawyer from Charlottesville. He came into the study with a stack of papers under his arm and put them on the table. Grandfather stood up and went to the table. He took up his pen and signed his name to one of the sheets. Benjamin came and signed

The Lost Stories

his name, too. Then Mr. Marlowe signed.

"Well, it is done," said Grandfather. "I am a poor man, but the happiest on earth."

Grandfather hugged Benjamin and Gracey together. He hugged Mr. Marlowe and Melinda together. He hugged Hannah all by herself, then turned to me and opened his arms. I jumped right in. Grandfather huffed as if I were a cannon ball. I told him that for a moment I thought that he was not such an old man, but perhaps I was mistaken. He said he was not old at all but that I had eaten half the wedding cake. I did not say anything to that, for I think it was true.

Grandfather set me down and kneeled in front of me. He pressed the key back into my hand.

"Everything is yours, Jenny. I've given Mariglenn to Benjamin and Gracey, but all else I give to you. You will learn what this means as time goes on. Mr. Marlowe will help you understand some things and if anything should happen to Mr. Marlowe, then you can talk to Mr. Wallace. But no one will be able to answer all your questions.

"I will tell you that everything is in the desk. But the desk has many keys. You have the green tasseled key, which means you have the desk. You must pass the key down to one of your children.

"Mr. Marlowe has all the other keys to the desk. He will administer the keys to you according to the instructions in these papers that I have signed. His children will administer the keys to your children. Your family will always have the desk, but Mr. Marlowe's family will always administer the keys. Do you understand, Jenny?"

"Not really," I told Grandfather.

"Good. It is best you are not troubled with it now. I pray it is never a burden to you and indeed it need never be if you can cast it aside without looking back."

"Is there anything in the desk that will help Mother?" I asked.

"If there is Jenny, you would be the one to find it. Your mother is caught in a fearful place between two worlds. She feels there is little to look forward to. She yearns for the past and is often looking backward as she tries to walk ahead."

"Is that why she often falls down?"

"I suppose it is," answered Grandfather.

Hannah went with me back to my room and tucked me into bed.

Katie was sound asleep.

"Isn't she wonderful?" I said to Hannah.

"Yes, she is," said Hannah. "Which reminds me of that whooping I owe that uncle of yours."

"Do not whoop him too hard," I told her.

"You're a wonder yourself, Jenny Sweetness."

I looked at the green tasseled key in the moonlight. I wondered what I would do with all the best things in the world.

"Hannah, what do you want in all the world?"

"What I want is in another world. There's too much fightin' and carryin' on in this world. Too many folks gettin' hurt."

"Isn't there anything you want in this world?"

"I want to see you on your wedding day and hold your first little baby."

"If it is a baby girl I will name her Hannah."

"It won't be a girl, Jenny. It's gonna be a little baby boy. I've already seen him. I just wanna get ahold of him and love on him awhile before he grows up and gets full of mischief and runs off into those mountains. That's all I want in this world, Jenny."

"When does the mischief set into a boy, Hannah?"

"All boys are born with the mischief already in them, but can't do nothing with it 'til they learn to run. So you gotta love 'em up before they can run. When they get so old they can't run, then a little sweetness comes in 'em. That's the way it is with boys."

"Does Grandfather have a little sweetness?"

"He can still run a little but I'm for certain that some sweetness is surely creep'n in to Colonel Pritcher."

"Hannah, will I see you in Heaven?"

"It wouldn't be Heaven if you and me wasn't there together, now would it? Now you stop asking questions. I know how you get."

"I love you, Hannah."

"I know it, Sweetness."

Hannah squeezed me goodnight and left me in the moonlight.

Publishers Note . . . continued

Thomas Marlowe Letter

September 18th, 2022

To Helen Freeman & David Burke at ODP,

In the summer of 1995, at the old Pritcher Estate, in the Virginia Highlands, we finally located the trunk containing many of the Pritcher / Marlowe journals and letters. Having been informed by my mother, many years ago, that such a repository must indeed exist, and likely at one of the family properties, I began to make more serious inquiries among my younger siblings and extended family when I returned from my overseas assignments and happily took an early retirement.

The *we* in this fortunate discovery is my wife Elaine, and our ever inquisitive and adventurous granddaughter, Morgan. In fact, ever since she was informed at the age of five or so, that the family was anxious to reclaim this heirloom, she never ceased to speculate earnestly regarding its whereabouts and pressed her parents and the rest of us to devote far more effort in *the search*.

There are three points of view (mine, Elaine's, and Morgan's) from which I draw this rendition of the events leading up to *The Find*, as we all now call it. I'm offering an account that has met everyone's approval. Elaine and I have combined ours based on our mutual recollections. Morgan has allowed me to insert an extract from her own childhood diary written less than a month after the event. I've provided photo copies of the original entries and we will allow you to edit them only in regards to spelling and punctuation and paragraph separations.

Morgan was staying the summer with us at Corrotoman, our Chesapeake Bay home, when my wife and I took her to Mariglenn on our annual 'escape the heat' visit to check in on our favorite farm.

We settled into the grand old place early Saturday afternoon. The weather was just as we hoped. Cool and dry for early August. The caretakers, whose families had been looking after Mariglenn since it was established in the 1830's, greeted us with their usual warm welcome and a wonderful meal derived entirely from produce off the estate.

Morgan wasted no time pressing the subject of the trunk (actually, she always referred to it as a *chest*, as we supposed that term attached more mystery and romance to the object in her mind). At this point I'd ruled out Mariglenn as the location of the family records.

I had inquired with Jack Green, the house manager, more than once before, and the answer was the same: "No recollection of finding anything in the manor house or the many outbuildings of that description."

After our late lunch we all went out with Jack to tour the farm and especially to see the new trout farming operation that was soon to be ready for action. Morgan said she needed to use the bathroom and would catch up with us. I honestly assumed she'd met up with Elaine in the pony stables but this turned out not to be the case. When we returned to the manor house a few hours later Morgan was already there in the kitchen eating another piece of pumpkin cheese cake. When asked where she'd been all this time she said she was, "just playing around the place."

Later that evening, Morgan was insistent on choosing which of the bedrooms she would sleep in. She selected the one in the far southwest corner on the second floor, which was suspicious since that room was as far away as possible from the master suite where she knew her grandmother and I would be sleeping.

Sometime, well after midnight, a powerful thunderstorm ripped through the region. I understand that tornadoes touched down in Covington twenty miles to the south and hailstones as big as lemons pelted much of Bath and Highland Counties. We were alone in the manor house when the power went out. I fumbled in the dark to light a few candles, which were scattered throughout the room in brass holders. We immediately went to check on Morgan, but she was not in her room. The covers and sheets lay twisted at the foot of the bed and one of the windows was wide open. The rain was pouring in over the sill and onto the floor. Wasting no more time than to shut the window, Elaine and I instinctively split up to search the adjoining rooms, both of us calling out for Morgan at the top of our lungs.

I thought it highly unlikely she would have tried to go out the window. Not that she wasn't inclined to such escapades, but because it was simply too far to the ground with nothing to climb on. But still, the fact of the open window conjured up awful images. I'm sure others will agree that the worst nightmare of any grandparent is for serious harm to befall a grandchild while in their care. You can imagine our relief, after a futile search of the upstairs rooms, when we heard the attic door creak open and saw our granddaughter descending the narrow staircase in her unicorn pajamas.

Morgan didn't bother to explain the open window or why she'd ventured into the attic. She greeted us excitedly with, "Pawpy . . . Gram . . . Come on. . . . I think I found something!"

We had no choice but to follow her since she'd already turned around and headed back up the steps. And as we did, it crossed my mind that we'd never been in the attic of the house before. I also wondered how Morgan got around up there in the dark.

Except for three exposed brick chimneys the cavernous room appeared entirely empty. Wide roughhewn boards covered the floor as far as we could see by the candlelight and hefty beams and rafters supported the steeply pitched roof. Lightning flashed through dormer windows as we followed Morgan toward the north end of the house.

Halfway in, a bolt of lightning struck so close to the house that there was no time separating the flash from the exploding thunder. Elaine jumped and dropped her candlestick on the floor, snuffing out the flame. I reacted with no less shock, and only by luck was able to hold on to our last source of light.

Morgan hardly flinched, but only stopped and turned to face us. "I know where the chest is," she declared.

We were well aware that Morgan was prone to very lucid dreams, and I suspected Elaine looked more uncomfortable with each passing second, but I figured at that point the quickest way to get everyone back in bed was to just humor the child and play along.

Morgan picked up the candle lying on the attic floor and

placed it back in the holder. She leaned the wick into my flame and relit the candle, and much like her intrepid little self she turned back around and continued her trek. We followed close behind as she headed decisively for the northeast corner of the attic. When she arrived, I figured we must be just above the master bedroom. The storm was still intense, rattling the windows and sending flashes of white blue light through the room.

Morgan stood dead still and pointed to a spot on the empty floor.

⁂

Morgan's Diary Entry*

The pumpkin thing dessert at the mountain farm is really good. But after I had my first one I needed to look all around in the big house. I didn't want Pawpy and Gram to see everything I was doing because sometimes they don't let me do things I want to do, so I waited until they went outside with Mr. Jack. I knew this house would be a good place for the secret chest to be, but Pawpy said no it's not... and somebody already looked there. But I think grownups don't do everything as good as they say they did.

My pen is starting not to work so now I'm going to do red pencil.

Gram says I won't get in trouble about anything I write down about this, just so it's all really what happened with no made up stuff, and also NO not telling about when I did things you're not allowed to do. I really really hope she means that and tells that to Mom and Dad. But there's things I did that aren't even the good part of what happened and would be dumb to write . . . like every time I was just walking and looking at things.

After the people left that cleaned up the kitchen I searched all over for a chest and didn't see one except a big one that only had blankets. I was thinking there should be a folded up map somewhere that tells where the secret chest was, so to find the map I needed to open up all the drawers and doors in all the furniture in almost the whole house, which is something you're not supposed to do . . . but I shut them again.

The last place I opened drawers was in the little bedroom at the very end. It had a little table next to the bed with just one drawer with nothing in it and one of those big things for hanging up clothes in. That had really pretty old dresses which would be neat to play with. Then there was a desk that you use to write on and maybe put your school stuff. I liked that. It had lots of little drawers on the top part and when I tried to open the one in the middle I got little tickly shocks, like what you get when you rub a balloon in your hair. So I didn't open that one yet but did all the others and nothing was in them. I tried the middle one again and it was empty too. But it looked like there was a picture in the bottom of it but it was hard to see what it was, so I took it all the way out to see better. I knew what that was. It was just like the tall standing up clock in the room downstairs with all the books and the really big fireplace.

This is too much writing today . . . like the biggest homework ever . . . so I'll maybe do more tomorrow.

Tomorrow,

The next thing was, I was looking at the picture of the clock that somebody drew in the bottom of the little drawer, with a pencil it looked like. And it was for sure the one in the downstairs. I was putting the drawer back in the desk, then I thought I saw something inside the hole where the drawer goes...and I did see something. It was in the far back hanging on a tiny nail. It was one of those olden keys. I put my hand in and got it out. That was a really good place to hide a key. I was thinking about why someone would hide that key there, and why someone would draw the picture of the big clock there. Then I had an idea that I should go down and look at that clock again.

This is the really good part that shows I'm good at finding things that no one else can.

I went to the room where the clock was. I think it had the same time it had before. I saw it had a place for a key in a door under from where the clock part was. I thought the desk in the far bedroom was giving me a secret message to open the clock door with the key. And the secret message was right and the key opened it. Inside it had strings and big heavy metal things hanging on the strings. Also there was a long part that can swing back and forth with a big round metal thing on the end, and I think that can make it tick tock.

I thought the secret chest could not be inside there because it was too small inside. I put my head in to look all around inside because maybe there would be a folded up treasure map, but there was nothing so I thought I was wrong about everything which made me a little mad at the clock so I hit the swinging tick tock thing maybe too hard because it banged on the sides going back and forth. When it was doing that I saw there was something drawn on the wood behind where the round thing was hanging before I hit it. And it was just like a map, so that's how I knew where the secret chest would be.

And because of all that good and smart work I did I thought I should have another piece of the pumpkin dessert. And I knew it would be in the old fridge. Then Pawpy and Gram came back when I was eating and I thought I didn't want to tell them much yet.

When it was bedtime I brought my suitcase and backpack to the room where I found the key because I wanted to look more at stuff in that room and it was the closest to where you can go up in the attic. After Pawpy and Gram said goodnight to me I waited some. I did probably go to sleep a little but it was too hot in that room for sleeping. I got up and opened the window all the way. I could see the stars really good for a while but then some clouds came. I thought I couldn't go to sleep anyway and also couldn't wait for the morning to get the chest.

I thought maybe I should wake up Pawpy and Gram and tell them. I went to their room at the far other end but then changed what I wanted to do. I wanted to go up in the attic and be sure I was right because old people do not like to wake up at night for no reason, but just to go pee.

EVERYTHING!!! is OLD!!! in that house and the light switch for the attic didn't even look like a light switch but I thought it might be and I pushed it up. I saw some light under the door at the top of the stairs so I knew it worked. The door was noisy to open and the room up there was super huge....gigantic huge, but there was no stuff up there. I went to the place at the other end that I thought the map in the clock was showing me to go. Maybe I was wrong about it, so I looked real close at other places because I betted I would find another map drawing on the wood on the floor.

I was looking for a long time and was thinking if I was going to get mad. I WAS getting mad but I went back to the first place. There was no drawing or anything. But then I saw something maybe a little bit funny. The other boards on the floor were all very long, then another long board, and you could see where they hit together. At the place where I thought the map was showing me there were two small boards about as long as me next to each other that went to wall near a chimney. I did some jiggling around with those boards and they jiggled a weensy bit.

I started hearing the rain but that was okay. I tried to make the first board come up but then I thought they were stuck to each other. Then there was some lightning and thunder, but that was okay too because I like it. Then the light went out. I thought probable because it was old. Now I wanted Pawpy and Gram to help me, but not because I'm afraid of the dark like some other kids.

I just waited for a lightning to come and I could see to

walk for some steps . . . and I kept doing that . . . then I got to the door and opened it and Pawpy and Gram were right there with candles which was just what I needed. So I told them I really found something.

So they came up for me to show them and we had a super big boomer lighting right next to the house. Then I got to get a candle to show them where the jiggly boards were.

I think Pawpy believed me but maybe Gram didn't. Pawpy tried real hard to get the boards up but he was pulling at the wrong end. I told him to do it from the end at the wall because I saw it move there. I told him to get off the boards and stop holding them down. I also told him I thought the nails there were fakey and didn't really go through. When Pawpy did what I told him to do the boards moved just a little, and everyone was surprised except me. Pawpy got his fingernails in real good and got the boards to come up a bit so I could get my hand in. Then we just lifted it up. It was two boards stuck together. The secret chest was right there and everyone could see it. It was pretty heavy but we still got it out. Now everyone knows to do stuff I say.

Morgan Marlowe

---

* **Publisher's Note:** Titled in the *Thomas Marlowe Letter* as "Morgan's diary entry as she recorded it that summer." Minor grammatical edits applied by the publisher.

Letter to Marlowe-Pritcher Descendants

November 20th, 2022

From: Thomas Marlowe III, Trustee for the Preservation of the Marlowe-Pritcher Mariglenn Estate

To: Descendants from the union of Oliver Marlowe and Jenny Habledean Pritcher

Dear Family (numerous and scattered abroad),

You may be wondering why I (on the advice of Estate counsel) have included this family letter with great-grandma Jenny's journals. Simply put, it's about control. We took preemptive control of the journals and how they are to be used for the benefit of the preservation of Mariglenn. We believe this is the best way to tether the Journals' publication with Estate guidance, deeming our approach the most efficient and safest.

Due to the prolific and widespread nature of the Marlow-Pritcher descendants (some who I don't even know and many yet to be born), it would have been nearly impossible to track you down. It was unreasonable to expect you to travel in from around the world and review the holdings in person. We cannot risk distributing them in electronic form, either. Who knows where and how they might promulgate haphazardly in the age of social media. We've already been stung once, over twenty five years ago, by my careless handling of the find. You have my utmost, sincere apology for that mistake.

Controlled releases should preempt any future lawsuits and family divisions that might come about by unauthorized leakages of the works. Over the last twenty-five plus years, we've tracked down and retrieved many of our invaluable family artifacts and works attributed to your ancestors. Have we located everything?

Not quite.

Although we were able to locate several journals where strange gaps appeared in great-grandma Jenny's journal entries (from the original find), we don't know . . . what we don't know. You can be the judge of that. Whether additional entry gaps indicate a missing journal is only speculation.

Great-grandma was obviously a prolific writer who was devoted to her art, and as we like to joke amongst ourselves, *got quite a charge from it*.

But a serious fact remains: Where we originally suspected gaps (and/or sparse journal entries), we vigilantly chased down the likely suspects and recovered several *'mishandled'* journals. The two that the estate published actually fall into this category.

The timing of this publication came about because we believe we have, in all likelihood, secured a majority of the most valuable works. We either physically reclaimed an artifact into the Mariglenn Estate Trust, or we are comfortable knowing that a particular artifact is safe, though not fully in our control. For example, one particular artifact was traced to the collections of a prestigious institution (to remain unnamed). We do not want to draw attention to it, but continue to track it in the unlikely event it is deaccessioned and placed at auction. Several artifacts have been traced to the holdings of a prominent family abroad, and here again, we will continue to track these artifacts while not drawing attention to them.

Per my apology, I am not blind to my previous mishandling of the initial find that led to the disappearance of several of these journals. Elaine and I had employed the expertise of a local furniture restoration business in Monterey, VA (not far from Mariglenn). We had yet to open the chest as I could not free its vintage lock mechanism without damaging it. We left the chest with the establishment overnight. Over the ensuing years, we realized our mistake and suspected some journals may have been pilfered. Through the efforts of the Mariglenn Estate legal counsel, two journals were recovered via a series of negotiations that took place over the course of a decade.

I pray that you show understanding in this matter and hope you've enjoyed the first installment of Great-grandma Jenny's journals. You are of course welcome (by appointment) to inspect them in person at Mariglenn per Estate guidelines (e.g., no picture taking, etc.).

Sincerely,

Thomas Marlowe III

Made in the USA
Columbia, SC
19 January 2023